BookEnds
Alpha & Omega

A Fable for All Seasons

by

Kirsten E.A. Borg

Cover Design & Computer Editor: Elisabeth Borg-Bowman

Order this book online at www.trafford.com
or email orders@trafford.com

Most Trafford titles are also available at major online book retailers.

Note for Librarians: A cataloguing record for this book is available from Library and Archives Canada at www.collectionscanada.ca/amicus/index-e.html

Printed in Victoria, BC, Canada.

ISBN: 978-1-4269-0159-1 (Soft)
ISBN: 978-1-4269-0161-4 (e-book)

We at Trafford believe that it is the responsibility of us all, as both individuals and corporations, to make choices that are environmentally and socially sound. You, in turn, are supporting this responsible conduct each time you purchase a Trafford book, or make use of our publishing services. To find out how you are helping, please visit www.trafford.com/responsiblepublishing.html

Our mission is to efficiently provide the world's finest, most comprehensive book publishing service, enabling every author to experience success. To find out how to publish your book, your way, and have it available worldwide, visit us online at www.trafford.com

Trafford rev. 06/22/2009

Trafford PUBLISHING www.trafford.com

North America & international
toll-free: 1 888 232 4444 (USA & Canada)
phone: 250 383 6864 • fax: 250 383 6804 • email: info@trafford.com

The United Kingdom & Europe
phone: +44 (0)1865 487 395 • local rate: 0845 230 9601
facsimile: +44 (0)1865 481 507 • email: info.uk@trafford.com

10 9 8 7 6 5 4 3 2 1

Contents

Prologue

WHEN I was 10 – *before the summer storm of adolescence – I saw the world with crystal clarity. I could see that some things were true – and that others were false. Not because anyone told me so, but because I just knew.*

When I was 60 – *in the calm haven of late autumn – I started to remember what I had forgotten while a woman on active duty. But now I am wiser, and can put the Truth of childhood in the context of all that I have learned since.*

When I was a child, *a pair of bookends sat on my father's desk. On one was carved the letter 'Alpha' , on the other 'Omega' – the beginning and end of the Greek alphabet. Those bookends are now on* *my* *desk, a reminder that the Beginning and End must join together to protect the Circle of Life.*

Part I
Alpha

Chapter 1

The Nerd

THE ALARM clock rang just as Valkira was jumping her black stallion over the fence. The corral in the backyard was full of several breeds of horse, who all whinnied in welcome.

She opened her eyes reluctantly, and rolled over on her back. Staring at the ceiling, she tried to think of a good reason to face what was sure to be another unpleasant day. Then she remembered that today she was giving her oral report in History class. She had been researching it for weeks, and was eager to see Ms. Anthony's reaction. Unlike her other Social Studies teachers, Ms. Anthony was not a coach and had actually admitted being a feminist. That she was also young and pretty had temporarily spared her from the flak for which she would otherwise have been a target.

Valkira dressed quickly in the outfit she had carefully chosen to illustrate her report. After buckling her overalls and pulling on her new cowboy boots, she fixed her hair in two Indian-style braids, and fastened a hippie-headband around her forehead. Around her neck hung a medallion with a peace sign.

Clomping downstairs in the slightly oversized boots, she sat down at the breakfast table as unobtrusively as she could. Her father, as usual, was hidden behind his newspaper.

"Harold dear, how do you want your eggs?" asked her mother, as usual fluttering about the kitchen making busy, industrious noises.

"Anything will be fine, Millicent dear," said her father absently.

"I could scramble them – oh, but there's no milk." Millicent had already been out jogging, but her stylish grey exercise suit was totally without sweat. And her hair was still perfectly combed.

"Then fry them," replied Harold.

"Sunny side up?"

"Whatever."

"Corn oil or olive oil?"

"Just put enough salt on them."

"Now Harold, you know too much salt is bad for your blood pressure."

"Yes, Millicent." There was an edge to Harold's voice.

"Oh, we're all out of cooking oil."

"Then use butter."

"Harold, you <u>know</u> that's bad for your cholesterol."

Harold rattled his newspaper. "Millicent, either make the damn eggs or give me some damn cereal!"

"Shall I cook oatmeal or do you want cold cereal?" twittered Millicent, undeterred.

Sighing, Harold turned the page of his newspaper.

Millicent's attention was fortunately diverted by Bradford entering the kitchen. Bradford was Valkira's older brother. He was in high school, and a very popular jock. As usual, he was carrying some kind of ball. Valkira wasn't sure which one – he was on all the teams. As always, she wondered why there had to be so many different shapes and sizes for what was essentially the same game.

Tiffany, Valkira's older sister, bounced into the room after Bradford. Tiffany was also in high school, and a very popular cheerleader. As usual, she was shaking her pom-poms. As always,

Valkira wondered why jumping about and yelling for all those silly ball-games bestowed so much status.

While Tiffany and Bradford chattered excitedly about whatever Big Game was scheduled for the weekend, Valkira quietly poured cold cereal into her bowl; she did not want to risk having to make up her mother's mind about what to eat.

While Tiffany and Millicent were engaged in the egg controversy, Valkira accidentally dropped her spoon. She silently cursed her clumsiness as both of them suddenly remembered she was there.

"Mother!" gasped Tiffany, scandalized. "Look what she's wearing!!!"

"This is my History costume!" replied Valkira defensively. "I'm giving my report today, and this is part of it."

"How could such a dumb outfit be homework!"

"It's about the American Frontier, and how all the fighting between the cowboys and farmers and Indians might have been prevented."

"Hey, I think the Cowboys and Indians are playing next week!" interjected Bradford.

Valkira stared at her brother, afraid that he might not be joking.

"What time?" asked Harold, from behind his newspaper.

Oh Lord, they're serious.

Millicent, meanwhile, had recovered her composure. "Valkira dear," she began in her ultra-sweet lady voice, "I'm sure your History teacher doesn't expect such graphic illustration."

Valkira – as always when her mother used that tone – felt like gagging.

"Why don't you change into those new designer jeans I bought for you last week."

"But Tiffany is always prancing around in her little cheerleader skirt, and Brad is always wearing some stupid uniform," argued Valkira stubbornly. "Why can't I wear my History uniform?"

"Oh, but dear, that's different." Millicent's voice was unruffled, but her face was flushed. "It's an honor for Tiffie and Braddy to wear their uniforms."

"If Bratty's coach told him to come to school naked, I bet you'd let him!"

"Valkira, that's enough," said Harold from behind his newspaper. "Go change your clothes!"

As Valkira ran from the room, Tiffany stuck out her tongue.

Valkira slammed the door to her bedroom as two hot tears rolled down her cheeks. Slowly she walked to her closet and took out the new jeans. The price tag was still attached. Glancing at it, she gasped. How could anyone pay that much for a stupid label! *They're just jeans!*

Remembering that she did, after all, consider jeans a sensible garment, Valkira regretfully took off her costume. The new jeans were fashionably tight and very uncomfortable. Even worse, the waist band was several inches below her waist. Irritated, she pulled the matching T-shirt over her head; it, too, was very tight and ended several inches above her waist.

Exasperated, she looked in the full-length mirror on the door of her closet. Between the shirt and the jeans were several inches of bare flesh. Her belly button glared angrily from an unattractive fold of stomach fat. The low-cut shirt hung straight on her flat chest and had absolutely no cleavage to display. Valkira sighed. Her round little body and long skinny legs were never intended for clothes such as these.

I look ridiculous!!!

Valkira suddenly burst out laughing.

And saw herself in the mirror again. *I look OK when I'm laughing.*

Taking a long cardigan out of a drawer, Valkira shrugged and went back down to the kitchen.

This time, Millicent and Tiffany looked at her with embarrassed pity.

"Valkira dear, maybe you should go on a diet," said Millicent patronizingly. "Tiffie dear, you could help her with that, couldn't you?"

"Of course," replied Tiffany, even more patronizingly. "But you'll have to work at it. It's harder for someone like <u>you</u> to look attractive."

Valkira liked Tiffany better when she merely stuck out her tongue.

"You look like a stuffed sausage!" guffawed Bradford.

"Now Braddy, don't be unkind," scolded Millicent. "Valkira can't help it if she's not athletic like you and Tiffie.

"And Bratty and Spiffie can't help it if they don't get A's like I do!" Valkira's chin jutted belligerently.

"Oh now, dear, there's more to life than just studying," gushed Millicent with disgustingly saccharine maternal concern. "Maybe we could take you to a doctor to help you lose weight."

"Yeah, maybe there's a pill for being fat!" Bradford snorted and bulged out his cheeks.

"Valkira is not fat. She's just ten years old," said Harold from behind his newspaper. "She'll grow out of it."

There was a stunned silence. Such a firmly stated opinion did not usually issue from Harold and his newspaper. Taking advantage of the moment, Valkira threw on her cardigan, grabbed her book bag, and left for school.

Ω Ω Ω

It wasn't a good day at school. But it wasn't an entirely bad one, either.

The History report was definitely an A+ with Ms. Anthony, who asked lots of questions and tried to get the class to join in. Unsuccessfully. Valkira wasn't sure if they hadn't understood, or just weren't interested. That was one of the worst things about being the only 10-year-old at Jane Addams Junior High School.

She never seemed to understand where the other kids were at. But at least they hadn't laughed at her, like when Theodore gave his report.

Theodore was short and skinny and wore glasses. Even Valkira thought he was a nerd. But a nice nerd. And probably a smart one. She knew that he, at least, had understood her report. He told her so after class, and then ran off, blushing, before she could return the compliment. What he had said was good, but how he had said it was painful to witness. Valkira was glad that she could at least speak to a group without falling apart like Theodore did. Ms. Anthony had done her best to ease his embarrassment, but there was only so much a teacher could do with a bunch of junior high kids.

For the millionth time, Valkira wondered if skipping grades had been such a good idea. Granted, Eleanor Roosevelt Elementary School had been boring and unchallenging. But classes here were even more boring and almost as unchallenging. The teachers weren't as nice, and the other kids were just as dumb. At least at Eleanor Roosevelt, she had been admired – albeit not understood. Here she was mostly ignored – and even more lonely.

But at least no one picked on her. They all knew she was smarter than they were. Much, much smarter. And that grudging respect cast a shield around her that protected as well as isolated. The wall was breached only occasionally by students desperate for 'help' with their homework.

"Hi," said Ashley, behind her in the lunch line of the school cafeteria. "Nice jeans." Ashley was one of the popular girls who had a big chest and was a cheerleader. She was an 8th-grader and didn't usually stand anywhere near Valkira. It wasn't hard to guess what was coming.

"Say, could I take a look at how you did Problem 13 of tomorrow's Algebra assignment? I can't seem to get that one right."

Valkira knew very well that she was really asking to copy, and answered as she usually did. "Well, I haven't finished it myself."

Though they both knew she had finished the entire assignment in only half the allotted class time.

"Oh, please!" Ashley looked genuinely distressed. "If I don't pass this quarter, they're going to put me back in Basic Math!"

Which even Valkira knew was a fate worse than death for a cheerleader. They weren't expected to get A's, but to be demoted to a 'retarded' class was unthinkable.

"I could show you how to do it," Valkira volunteered impulsively. "It's really not that hard."

"Oh, could you?" Genuine relief flooded Ashley's pretty face.

"Sure. How about during study hall, in the student lounge?"

Ashley's face fell, as she looked quickly over her shoulder to see if anyone had noticed whom she was talking to.

Valkira saw the look. "OK, how about in the library?"

"Yes, that'll be great!" They both knew the popular kids never went near the library. "See you then. And those really are nice jeans."

Valkira sighed, and took her tray over to a table in the corner and sat down alone. In the center of the cafeteria, she saw Ashley join the Popular Girls. They were all in their little cheerleader skirts – and were pointing and snickering at a small 7th-grader whose clothes were shabby and very unfashionable. She was skinny and pale and had mouse brown hair – and was desperately looking for a place to hide.

One of the 9th-graders stuck out her foot and deliberately tripped the girl, who dropped her tray with a crash. Everyone cheered and applauded. The girl frantically fumbled to retrieve the spilled food.

A wave of indignation swept over Valkira. She stood and walked quickly to where the mortified girl was struggling to get up. "Here," said Valkira, offering her hand and helping her to her feet.

The girl hurriedly picked up her tray and what was left of her lunch.

"Come on, you can sit with me," said Valkira. "And YOU," she continued, turning to the 9th-grade girl who had done the tripping, "can clean up the mess you made!"

The cafeteria was unnaturally still as she turned and walked back to her lunch.

"Thanks," said the small pale girl as she sat down across from Valkira. "My name's Ophelia. My Mom and I just moved here. This is my first day, and I don't know anyone."

"Well, now you know me. My name's Valkira. I don't have anyone to eat lunch with either, so I'm glad to meet you."

During 7th Period, on her way to the library to meet Ashley, she collided with Theodore. He was running out of the boys' bathroom, and his hair was soaking wet. Valkira had occasionally overheard her brother and his friends laughing about 'pranks' played on nerdy kids who didn't have a pack to run with. So she knew that some of the bigger boys had probably been flushing Theodore's head in the toilet. Ms. Anthony's classroom was across the hall; Valkira grabbed his arm, pulled him into the fortunately empty room, and shut the door.

When the hooting gang had disappeared down the hall, Theodore relaxed. Pulling his glasses from his pocket, he managed a weak grin. "At least I was able to hide these before they caught me. Last time, my glasses almost got flushed, too."

"Does this happen a lot?"

"As often as they can catch me – which is less than it used to be." Theodore put his glasses back on. "Fortunately, they're not too smart."

"Have you reported them?"

"What good would that do? There aren't enough teachers to watch the bullies all the time," shrugged Theodore philosophically. "And Principal Cox thinks 'boys-being-boys' will make men of us."

"That's disgusting!" exclaimed Valkira indignantly. "Surely something can be done!"

"I keep hoping they'll get bored – and that I'll survive until high school," he sighed. "I hear it's not so bad there."

"Yeah, me too." Valkira also sighed. "Hopefully by that time, they'll have grown up or dropped out."

"Meanwhile, maybe we can watch each other's backs." Theodore glanced nervously at the door.

"Good idea." Valkira opened the door and peeked cautiously into the hall. "I think it's safe now." She hesitated. "Well, I'm supposed to meet someone in the library."

"That's OK. I'll just wait here for Ms. Anthony," said Theodore, heading for the desk farthest out of sight from the door. "See you tomorrow . . . . And thanks. I owe you one."

Valkira walked carefully down the hall toward the library, thankful that girls usually considered flushing anything in toilets too messy. And was momentarily grateful that her unique status as resident child prodigy usually shielded her from the kind of meanness inflicted on Ophelia at lunch. Valkira herself was so different that she was not even on the Junior High radar most of the time. That was lonely, but maybe there were worse things than being left alone.

Ashley was waiting for her at a table behind a big bookcase, still nervous that someone cool might spot her in the most un-cool possible place with the school's most un-cool student.

Valkira sat down and took out her Algebra book, and turned to the assigned word problems. "Let's see what you've done so far."

"Well – ah . . . ." Ashley looked embarrassed.

"Haven't you done ANY of them?"

"Well – ah . . . . No."

"Why not?" demanded Valkira.

"Because I don't get it, OK?!!!" replied Ashley angrily. "Not everyone's a genius like you!"

"You don't have to be a genius to do word problems," insisted Valkira. "They're really not that hard."

"Easy for you to say," sniffed Ashley. "But how do you get numbers out of all those silly words?"

"Think of it this way," replied Valkira, considering how to answer a question that seemed so obvious to her – but obviously not to Ashley. "When Ms. Fleur gives us a test in French class, what is she asking us to do?"

"To translate, of course," answered Ashley, who always got A's in French. "French into English, English into French, depending."

"That's what you have to do with a word problem – translate the words into numbers."

"Ohhhh," said Ashley, as light dawned. "But why would anyone want to do such a stupid thing?"

"Because sometimes numbers are simpler than words."

"I like words better."

"Sometimes, so do I," agreed Valkira. "But knowing the language of numbers helps you understand some important ideas that are hard to translate into words."

"Kind of like translating French poetry into English?"

"Yeah, something like that."

"But French isn't really any harder to figure out than English – once you know it. Why are numbers so much harder than words?"

"They aren't." Valkira shook her head. "Some people just want you to think so."

"But why?"

"I'm not sure – but I think it's maybe because the stupider they can make you feel, the smarter they can believe they are."

"Wow," said Ashley, with genuine admiration. "How do you think of all this stuff?"

"I just do," shrugged Valkira.

"You are <u>so</u> lucky to be <u>so</u> smart!"

"It's not always so great," said Valkira ruefully. "Sometimes it's pretty lonely. No one ever invites <u>me</u> to sit at their lunch table."

"Really?"

"Would you invite me to yours?"

Ashley was silent. "No, I guess not." She hesitated. "But sometimes I don't want to sit there, either."

"Like today?"

"Yeah. That was mean. I felt bad about what happened to that girl."

"Then why didn't you say something?"

Ashley again hesitated. "Because then I wouldn't be allowed at the center table, either."

"So?"

"Haven't you ever wanted to be there?"

This time, Valkira was silent. "Well, yes, sort of – maybe sometimes. But I'm so different I know that'll never be an option."

"So you can do whatever you want," Ashley said in a rush. "Sometimes I wish I had that kind of freedom!"

When the bell rang, Ashley jumped up and almost ran to the library door.

Valkira gathered her books and headed for the band room, still marveling that a popular cheerleader with a big chest should actually envy her. Ashley, she knew, would never say 'Hi' to her in the hall. But maybe this was better.

Seeing several band members already going outside, Valkira quickly got her cymbals from the percussion cabinet and followed. She played oboe in the concert band – which of course was not a marching instrument – so during football season she was given cymbals, and tried to clang them as often as she could. Valkira enjoyed the marching itself; on days when the drill went well, it was rather like dancing. Staying in step and in line and in tune was more difficult than what the football players and cheerleaders did at the games. That no one seemed to recognize this, and instead took the band for granted, Valkira resented mightily.

"C'mon, c'mon, double-time!" shouted Mr. Marcheson, herding the last of his band out onto the football field for one of the rare times they were allowed to practice there. The band was to compete in a marching contest next month. Mr. Marcheson hoped that winning it would persuade the School Board to buy some new sousaphones. The old ones were dented and had broken valves.

Valkira lined up on the 50-yard-line with the rest of the percussion section. The drum major blew his whistle, and the drummers began their syncopated cadence. Valkira was glad she hadn't let Mr. Marcheson talk her into playing saxophone for marching band. She had insisted that it would ruin her oboe embouchure. Which was true. But mostly she didn't think she could play musical notes while simultaneously executing all the complicated maneuvers. Just clashing her cymbals on every 8th beat was hard enough. Which was why Band was her most challenging class. And her favorite.

It was a hard practice. They had rehearsed all the components inside several times. But putting it all together out on the big field was difficult. Mr. Marcheson's whistle blew constantly, stopping and starting them at various points in the maneuver. Finally, they were able to get through the whole drill without stopping.

"OK, that's more like it!" shouted Mr. Marcheson through his bull-horn. "One more time, and I think we've got it!"

They were halfway through when Valkira felt something hit one of her cymbals. Then saw something bounce off the bass drum next to her, and get stuck in the bell of the sousaphone behind her. Notes went sour and the cadence broke, as a shower of footballs rained down on the band. The football team stood on the sidelines, pitching balls and laughing, cheering whenever they hit one of the instruments.

The football team wasn't supposed to take possession of the field until after school. But here they were – early as usual. Mr. Marcheson and the football coach were yelling at each other – as usual. Finally Principal Cox appeared, and broke it up. After a few minutes, the football coach looked smug and the band director furious. Valkira knew that the band – once again – was being thrown off the field during their one short practice period per week. As they all walked back to the band room and put away their instruments, Valkira was not the only one who was mad.

She left school that day, seething with the injustice of it all. And fantasized about the dreadfully humiliating things she wished she could inflict on the football team. And even more, on the despicable Principal Cox and his stupid minions, who thought tossing balls about was the most important thing in the world!!

Ah, yes. Someday. Someday she would even the score.

Chapter 2

The SuperHero

After school, Valkira headed for her grandmother's house, which was only a few blocks out of her way home. Grandmère Minerva conveniently lived close enough for Valkira to walk, but far enough to discourage unnecessary visits from the rest of her family.

On the outside, Grandmère Minerva's house looked like the other houses on the block – though its blue paint was maybe a little brighter, and the brown trim had a nearly indiscernible orange tint. The small front yard was neatly mowed, with just a few dandelions. Two slightly asymmetrical bushes flanked the steps, and a small bed of flowers was trying – almost successfully – to look obedient.

On the inside, however, was another world. Floor-to-ceiling shelves were lined with books on every conceivable subject; a harpsichord with a half-finished cabinet was stacked high with music and surrounded by several other musical instruments. Original artwork by several artists filled the walls, bric-a-brac from all over the world cluttered the tables, whimsical mobiles hung from ceiling murals. Brightly-colored sitting cushions covered handmade oriental rugs, beaded curtains covered the windows, and dragon-shaped candle holders sat on the sills.

Grandmère Minerva greeted Valkira with a firm hug. Though no longer slim, she was not fat – but very strong. She was dressed in one of her long brown gowns, which flowed elegantly and matched her thick dark hair, streaked with silver that sometimes looked gold. Around her neck was a gold chain, from which hung the round medallion she always wore; it was set with a large blue sapphire the color of her eyes. From her pierced ears dangled golden spirals, and on her right ring finger she wore a band of artfully entwined silver and gold.

The house, as usual, smelled pleasantly of incense; classical music filled the rooms. Sometimes, on special occasions, it was jazz or – if she was meditating – New Age. Today, however, it was Bach; Grandmère Minerva was cleaning her kitchen, to which she returned to get refreshments.

While she waited, Valkira sat down on a brown velvet divan. It was crowned with a blue mesh canopy and adorned by two well-fed Siamese cats. Like her grandmother, they were no longer svelte – but still elegant.

"*Bonjour*," said Valkira politely.

"*Bonjour,*" replied Katya, graciously moving over, making it clear that she was doing Valkira a huge favor.

Koshka merely opened her eyes and allowed herself to be petted. She was the quiet one.

Grandmère Minerva returned with a tray of iced green tea and rice krispie bars.

"*Alors, mes chères,*" she said enthusiastically to the cats, "*Voilà Valkira!*"

"*Mais oui,*" said Katya, yawning.

Koshka nodded, also yawning, and crawled onto Valkira's lap.

Katya curled up next to Minerva and closed her eyes, one ear pointed toward Valkira, who was munching meditatively on a rice krispie treat.

"Well?" said Grandmère Minerva finally, putting on her listening face. The furrows on her forehead deepened with concentration.

"Why must they bother so much about what I wear?!" blurted out Valkira, looking up at her grandmother's clear blue eyes, which regarded her, as always, with complete attention. Small wrinkles radiating out of their corners gave them a wryly humorous cast.

"Because they worry so much about what they wear," replied Grandmère Minerva calmly. "And because what everyone else wears matters too much to them."

"But why can't they leave me alone?"

"They don't want you to embarrass them," replied Grandmère Minerva matter-of-factly. "And – yes – they're trying to protect you."

"From what?!" demanded Valkira.

"From being ridiculed by all the other people who worry too much about how they look."

"But that's silly!"

"Camouflage is useful to all animals sometimes." Minerva gently stroked Katya's sleek fur. "Looking like everyone else can sometimes save you from fighting when it doesn't matter."

"But you don't dress like everyone else!"

"At my age, you can get away with more," shrugged Minerva. "And by now, people expect me to be eccentric."

"I wish I was as old as you," grumbled Valkira.

"No, you don't," smiled Minerva. "Besides, it doesn't work unless you've lived all the ages in between."

"So I should just wear what they want me to?"

"For some occasions, why not? Why does it matter so much to you?"

"Because they're trying to make me something I'm not!"

"And what would the real you like to wear?"

"Well . . . " pondered Valkira, reaching very carefully for another rice krispie square so as not to startle Koshka, purring in her lap. "Something more exciting, with bright colors – and lots of sequins."

"Something that says who YOU are?"

"Yes! Exactly!"

"And who are you?"

"Someone who isn't like everyone else! Someone who just wants to be who she is! And who hates it when people are mean to people who are different!"

"Is that what happens at school?"

"Not to me, usually." Valkira shook her head. "I'm 'The Brain' and help them with their homework sometimes. Most of them don't especially like me, but they usually leave me alone. But they're really mean to some of the other kids."

"And you don't like that."

"It makes me mad! It's so unfair!"

"What can be done about it?"

"I wish I knew! Someone should defend them! They need a superhero!"

"Why don't you be their SuperHero?

"ME?!"

"Why not?"

"But . . . . I have no super-powers!"

"Yes, you do. You just don't see them."

Valkira thought about that. Her grandmother never lied.

"But . . . . then . . . . how do I find them?"

"A proper costume would help."

"You mean like my History costume?"

"Umm, sort of – but not just any costume." Grandmère Minerva stood up suddenly. "I think it's time we made your first real Costume!"

"*Mon Dieu!*" protested Katya loudly, her nap rudely interrupted.

Minerva went to her study and returned with several sheets of paper and a box of colored pencils.

"*Merde,*" said Koshka quietly, as Valkira, intrigued, removed the cat from her lap.

Valkira got to work, discarding one sketch after another. Chasing the crumpled wads of paper, the cats got into a fight. Katya, as usual, won and carried off her trophy to a bright blue cushion that matched her eyes perfectly. Posing herself artistically, she placed one paw on the disputed ball of paper.

Koshka glared at her. "*Zut!*" she hissed under her breath.

Minerva, however, had sharp ears. "*S'il vous plait, mes amis, regardez votre bouches!*" she said sternly.

Koshka retreated sulkily to a green pillow across the room.

Finally, after much drawing and coloring and conferring and discarding, Valkira triumphantly held up a sketch. "This is it!"

"Hmmm," said Minerva, looking carefully at the drawing. "I'll have to go shopping to get what we need to make it."

Twisting her long braid into a generous chignon, Minerva swirled a russet-colored cloak onto her shoulders and reached for her favorite hat. Of copper-colored felt, it was pinned up on one side with a silver crescent moon, which also fastened a bushy blue plume. Glancing in the mirror, she put the hat at a rakish tilt, and swept out the back door. Valkira followed eagerly.

Olga came bounding joyfully up to the porch, and sat obediently at Minerva's feet.

"Ah, dear *Tovarisch!*" exclaimed Minerva, scratching the dog's ears affectionately. "My loyal Comrade!"

"Яррф! Яррф!" replied Olga. A Siberian Husky with a deep throaty voice, she barked with a thick Russian accent.

Noting Minerva's traveling ensemble, Olga raced over to her dog dacha, which had a small onion dome on top. She soon emerged, pulling a sled whose silver wings matched her silver-grey fur. Tail wagging at top speed, she ran happily back to Minerva, who climbed into the sled and sat down on a pile of sable furs.

Minerva smiled and pointed toward the forest in back of the yard. And off they flew, over the top of the birch trees.

Valkira sat down to wait in her favorite chair. It was carved in the shape of a chubby dragon, and was surprisingly comfortable. Leaning back between his wings, Valkira gazed fondly at her grandmother's garden. It was a wild tangle of enthusiastically verdant bushes and trees and flowers no one else in town ever grew. And had probably never seen – or even heard of. Valkira herself had been unable to find any of them in any of the botany books in the library. Which made her love the garden all the more. The exotic plants were different each time she visited, and the flowers constantly changed colors before her eyes. Valkira marveled – as she always did – that though the garden was full of trees of all shapes and sizes, they all seemed happy to be together in Grandmère Minerva's garden. As they swayed contentedly to the music which always played from the back porch, Valkira dozed off.

After what seemed a very short time, Valkira saw the silver sled flying back over the trees, and watched as Olga skillfully landed next to the porch without a single bump.

"*Spasiba,* Olga," said Minerva as she stepped gracefully out of the sled, carrying several packages.

"Ярррф!" replied Olga, still grinning happily. She pulled the sled back to her dacha, and quickly returned to the porch.

"*Allons-y, mes chères,*" said Minerva, opening the door to let Katya and Koshka out.

"Ярррф!" said Olga tolerantly, sitting at Minerva's feet. She considered the cats disgracefully lazy and totally useless.

"*Miieux,*" replied Katya in polite catese, a language she rarely used. Koshka merely nodded – trying, with minimal success, to match Olga's tolerant mien. Both cats considered dogs in general disgustingly subservient, and Olga in particular a classless workaholic. With just a trace of condescension – calculated to elude Minerva's democratic eye – the cats stretched gracefully and curled up on the pillow between Valkira and her grandmother.

"ГрррЛ," growled Olga very quietly.

Minerva, meanwhile, opened the packages, which contained yards of purple lycra and silver satin, lots of sequins, and a silver motorcycle helmet.

"SuperHeroes should always wear safety helmets when they fly," shrugged Minerva, following her granddaughter's gaze. "It sets a good example."

"Am I going to fly?" wondered Valkira excitedly.

"That depends on what kind of SuperHero you need to be." And with that, Minerva began to measure and cut and sew, humming along with the stirring Wagnerian overture sounding forth from the porch speakers.

Valkira, too, hummed as she sewed countless sequins onto the unusual garments her grandmother was fashioning with fingers seeming to move at amazing speed. Though not as quickly, her own fingers also seemed to be flying.

When the costume was finished, the music stopped.

"Now, go try it on," smiled Minerva, laying the shiny garments over Valkira's arm. "Oh, and these go with it," she added, handing her a large shoe box.

Much later, Valkira appeared, clad in her new Costume. A bright purple unitard was overlaid by a short silver tunic with lightening bolts of purple sequins on the chest. Silver boots were on her feet, and a purple cape with silver sequin stars was fastened around her neck.

"And now, for the crowning touch!" beamed Minerva, placing the silver helmet on Valkira's head. Protruding from either side was a pair of small cow horns, painted purple and sprinkled with purple glitter.

"Well, what do you think?" asked Minerva, enormously pleased with her handiwork, as they both contemplated Valkira's reflection in the big mirror which had suddenly appeared on the porch.

"Well . . . .You don't think it's – ah – too much?" asked Valkira, trying to recognize the person she saw in the mirror.

"Too much?!! Oh, my dear, you should have seen some of the costumes I used to wear in my younger days!!!" Minerva got a far away look in her eyes and gently caressed the ring on her finger. "Particularly when I met your grandfather . . . ."

"What were they like?" Valkira asked quickly, always eager to hear about her grandmother's early life, especially the parts about the mysterious grandfather she'd never met.

"Well . . . . One of them was a gold lamé cat-suit, with a beaded headband of chartreuse peace signs . . . . And another had red patent leather boots – thigh-high, of course – and a red satin cape, lots of flowing hair . . . . And not much else." Minerva smiled nostalgically.

"Maybe someday you'll make a costume like that for me?"

"Not until you're older . . . . Much older!" Grandmère Minerva abruptly came back to the present. "And there will be considerably more coverage!"

Valkira continued to gaze at her reflection. She liked what she saw. Oh yes, she definitely did. "I look like ME!!!" she exclaimed, delighted.

"Of course you do! That's the whole point!" said Grandmère Minerva proudly. "And how do you feel?"

"Bigger. And stronger. And not afraid," replied Valkira, frowning slightly. "But how can clothes do that?"

"They can't," Grandmère Minerva shook her head. "It's the attitude that goes with them that counts. Your strength and courage have always been there. The Costume just helps you see it."

"Will other people see it, too?"

"Probably more easily when you wear the Costume."

"So if I want to be a SuperHero, I'll need to wear it?"

"It would help."

"But I can't wear this at home – or at school." Valkira's face fell.

"That's OK. Being a SuperHero is hard work. You'll need to rest in between and wear camouflage."

"But what do I do with the costume in between?"

"Go change your clothes, and I'll show you."

After a last look in the mirror, Valkira reluctantly did as she was told. She returned to the porch in her school clothes, her shoulders slumped.

"I don't feel like ME now," she sniffed.

"Here's something to help you focus your power." Grandmère Minerva handed her a ring with a silver dragon entwining a large amethyst.

"Oh, it's beautiful." Valkira slipped the ring on her finger and admired it.

"Now sit down and concentrate."

Valkira sat down in the dragon chair, leaned back against its wings and closed her eyes.

"Now remember what you saw in the mirror. See yourself as you did then," Grandmère Minerva said in a quiet, soothing voice. "Focus on that . . . . That's right . . . Focus . . . . What do you see?"

Valkira took a deep breath and looked into her mind. Gradually she began to see herself in the costume – first the bright purple unitard, covered by the short silver tunic with the purple lightening bolt. Then the silver boots appeared on her feet, and the purple cape with silver stars fluttering in the breeze. Finally, the helmet with the purple horns.

"Do you see it?"

"Yes. Yes, I do!"

"And how do you feel?"

"Big . . . . And strong . . . . And not afraid!" replied Valkira jubilantly. "And like ME!!!"

"Then that's how people will see you. When you want them to."

Valkira opened her eyes. And felt her strong self crash. "But now I'm just plain me again."

"Just plain you is merely a quieter version of YOU."

"If I close my eyes and focus, can I be ME again?"

"Yes, but you don't want to do it all the time," cautioned Grandmère Minerva. "Or you'll burn out."

"Can I do it once more before I go home?"

"Yes, of course," smiled Grandmère Minerva. "And I'll even give you a magic word to make it happen faster."

Valkira again leaned back and closed her eyes.

"Focus and visualize."

Valkira obeyed.

"Now repeat after me . . . . *Ohm* . . . . *Ohmm* . . . . *Ohmmm* . . . ."

"Ohm . . . . Ohmm . . . . Ohmmm . . . ." chanted Valkira.

Nothing.

"Ohm . . . . Ohmm . . . . Ohmmm . . . ."

Still nothing.

"Remember how you felt," said Grandmère Minerva encouragingly.

Valkira focused on that. *"Ohm . . . . Ohmm . . . . Ohmmm . . . ."*

Then, suddenly, there she was, in all her purple grandeur!

"Ярррф! Ярррф!" barked Olga joyously, running in circles around her. "Ярррф!"

"*Très bien!*" said Katya, leaping up to the top of the dragon chair.

"*Mais oui!*" said Koshka, in a rare moment of loquaciousness.

"VALKIRA the BRAVE!" Grandmère Minerva hugged her triumphantly. "Defender of the Picked-Upon!"

The Wagnerian Overture once more sounded forth.

Chapter 3

Shazam!

On Monday morning, Valkira got out of bed as soon as the alarm clock started ringing, eagerly anticipating the launching of her new super-persona. Dressing as neutrally as possible in a sloganless T-shirt and jeans that did not bare her midriff, she hurried down to breakfast.

Slipping unnoticed into her usual corner seat, Valkira reached for the cornflakes and looked around the table. Her father, as usual, was behind the *Wall Street Journal;* Bradford was bouncing whatever ball it was the season for, alternating backboards all over the kitchen. When he threw at the ceiling, Millicent interrupted the morning egg dialogue.

"Bradford dear, please stop. You'll break something."

Bradford grinned, and started aiming at Valkira's feet.

Tiffany excitedly flounced into the kitchen. "Mother, can we go downtown right after school today?" She had been nominated for Homecoming Queen and was swishing her little cheerleader skirt more snottily than usual. "Last year, most of the best dresses had already been sold by the time we got there."

"Of course, dear!" Millicent was as excited as Tiffany, and was gushing more than usual. "I'll write a note saying you have a dentist appointment, so we can get an early start!"

"But that's dishonest!" exclaimed Valkira, looking hopefully at her father's newspaper.

"Oh, just this once won't hurt anything," burbled Millicent. "Tiffie has to look her best at the coronation!"

"Since when is getting a stupid crown – without any power, yet – a good reason for lying?!" Valkira again looked at the *Wall Street Journal,* which was rattling slightly.

"Some people just don't understand what's important!" Tiffany sighed with unusually condescending exasperation.

"Oh, of course they do!" said Millicent. "Valkira dear, you're happy for your sister, aren't you?!"

Valkira grunted affirmatively. Actually, she was happy that Tiffany was happy. Despite everything, she wished she and her sister could be friends. "I hope you get to be Queen," said Valkira sincerely. "If that's what you want."

Harold turned the page of his newspaper and read on.

"Of course *it's* what I want!" Tiffany rolled her eyes. "Who wouldn't?!"

"It's what every girl wants!" seconded Millicent.

Valkira thought longingly about the wonderful Costume Grandmère Minerva had made for her, and was sorely tempted. . . . *But no, she said I should save it for really important stuff*. . . .

At that moment, Bradford's bouncing ball hit her foot. Hard.

"Ouch!" yelled Valkira. And then, more quietly, *"Ohm . . . . Ohmm . . . . Ohmmm."*

And suddenly, there she was, standing at the head of the family breakfast table, hands on hips and sequins glittering.

Valkira pointed the large purple ring on her finger at Bradford's ball, which flew out of his hands and crashed into the wastebasket.

"You're NOT going to wear THAT to school?!!!" gasped Millicent and Tiffany, *à deux.*

Valkira aimed her left horn at Millicent, who suddenly emitted a resounding and sustained fart. She then aimed her right horn at

Tiffany's nose, which immediately blossomed into an enormous zit.

And just before she ran out of the room, she aimed both horns at the *Wall Street Journal.* The newspaper disappeared and left Harold staring – with stunned surprise – at his family.

So THAT's what he looks like!

Ω Ω Ω

Valkira arrived at school a few minutes before the bell rang. She was back in her neutral blues, but in her pocket was a pair sunglasses. *Just in case I need to be incognito.*

In History class, it was Ophelia's turn to give her report. "A lot of the – uh – Wild West – uh – happened on land – uh – that we took from – uh – Mexico. They – uh – are still sort of mad at us – uh – because we started the – uh – Mexican War, but – uh – sort of blamed it on them."

Ophelia has a brain! Valkira was elated and gave her new friend an encouraging smile.

Ophelia's face became a less vivid shade of red, and she continued with less stammering.

Then Stacey started to giggle. Stacey wasn't a cheerleader, but she had the biggest chest in the whole school. She was therefore popular with the boys, and consequently followed by the popular girls.

Ms. Anthony glared at Stacey, who stopped giggling – but started yawning ostentatiously and gesturing rudely as soon as the teacher looked away. Some of her friends joined in.

Valkira was fortunately sitting in the back row. Ms. Anthony had put her there in hopes of breaking up a bothersome cluster of noisy boys. Silently she slipped on her sunglasses. The boys were too busy ogling Stacey's chest to notice.

"Ohm . . . . Ohmm . . . . Ohmmm . . . ." Valkira closed her eyes and chanted silently.

Suddenly she felt brave and strong, as she had in her Costume. But opening her eyes, she noted that the incognito had worked: no Costume – on the outside.

Good! I don't want to disrupt Ms. Anthony's class.

Aiming her purple dragon ring at Stacey, she closed her eyes again and focused. A HUGE fart exploded from Stacey and echoed around the classroom.

Stacey turned bright red and looked for a place to hide.

Everyone in the class – including Ms. Anthony – burst out laughing.

When the laughter finally subsided, and Ms. Anthony was wiping her eyes in between lingering giggles, Ophelia continued her report – minus the heckling and without stammering. When she was done, she flashed Valkira a knowing smile.

Valkira took off her sunglasses, wonderfully satisfied. *Wow! Justice feels great!*

After school, as she was putting her books in her locker, Theodore came pounding down the hall, fleeing from his usual gang of tormentors. Before Valkira could intervene, the bullies grabbed him and pushed him into the boys' bathroom.

Valkira put on her sunglasses and peeked in.

Theodore was being dragged, struggling, towards one of the stalls.

Valkira closed her eyes, chanted, and aimed her ring at the biggest boy.

Suddenly the toilet seat flew up and the toilet bowl spewed forth several buckets of water, totally drenching the leader of the gang. The lesser bullies hooted and pointed derisively at him.

Theodore wisely ducked out of the bathroom, completely dry, and took off down the hall.

Valkira walked away, humming.

The next day, in Gym class, a gaggle of popular girls were snickering and pointing at Ophelia's ragged gym shoes. This time the ringleader was Tracey, who had the second biggest chest in the whole school.

Valkira focused, chanted, and aimed.

A stupendous pimple appeared on Tracey's forehead, right between the eyes. Screeching, she ran back into the locker room.

Later that day, Valkira again encountered Theodore, running from the bullies in customary pursuit mode.

She focused, chanted, and aimed.

This time, several rolls of toilet paper shot out of the boys' bathroom, and wrapped up the lead bully like a mummy. While he was struggling to disentangle himself, Theodore bolted and vanished into Ms. Anthony's classroom across the hall.

By the end of the week, Valkira was exhausted.

The girls seemed to be getting the message. After casting several embarrassing farts and zits on various members of the popular clique, Valkira noted that Ophelia was – almost – making it through the day unharassed.

The bullies, however, appeared unable to grasp the cause-and-effect connection between their persecution of Theodore and the mysterious behavior of the toilets. Valkira had finally resorted to lining them all up before the urinals, which – with impressive military precision – simultaneously shot water at them. Some of the brighter bullies walked out of the bathroom that day with a small light bulb over their heads.

Valkira was encouraged, but no longer humming. Being a SuperHero was hard work.

"Of course it is!" said Grandmère Minerva, when Valkira stopped by to give a progress report. "Anything worth doing takes effort."

"But I can't be everywhere at once," sighed Valkira. "There are just too many mean kids."

"Then maybe it's time Valkira the Brave became more visible."

"But I can't wear my Costume in school," objected Valkira. "I'd get suspended for violating the dress code."

"Hmmph! That Principal Cox has no fashion sense," snorted Grandmère Minerva. "However, your point is well-taken. Perhaps a dramatic appearance to the school *en masse* would be more effective."

"Like – say – at the football game tomorrow?"

"Yes, yes! What a splendid idea!"

Grandmère Minerva and Valkira put their heads together and planned the formal debut of her career as Junior SuperHero. After the cats approved, Valkira went home. It was late and she had missed dinner. But so excited was she about the next day's spectacle, she wasn't even bothered as Millicent scolded her up the stairs.

Ω Ω Ω

Valkira slept late on Saturday morning. She was tired and needed to recoup her strength for the game that afternoon. When she finally arose, she put on her band uniform, and astounded Millicent by requesting eggs for breakfast, cooked in every possible way.

Valkira went to the game early, for a last-minute band rehearsal of the half-time show. The football players didn't want to wear themselves out before the game; the football field was therefore available without doing battle.

Mr. Marcheson was in a bad mood. The School Board had denied his request for a new sousaphone. And today the football team was wearing brand new uniforms. Their 'old' uniforms had been purchased just last year, whereas the band uniforms were ancient. Valkira had to bunch up her trousers with a big belt just to keep them from falling down; the cuffs of her jacket were frayed and the gold buttons tarnished. The rest of the band didn't look much better.

Valkira sat with the band during the 1st quarter and watched the football players fumble the ball and trip over their own feet. When the opposing team kicked the ball, the receivers even ran away from it. *If they're going to play such a stupid game, they should at least do it right!*

The cheerleaders were, admittedly, more coordinated than the football team. But it made Valkira sad to watch their plastic grins and exaggerated enthusiasm. Even worse were the suggestive movements whose meaning even Valkira knew they couldn't – or shouldn't – understand.

Toward the end of the 2nd quarter, the band lined up near the goal posts. The buzzer sounded, and the football players strutted off the field, some of them making snide remarks about band nerds as they passed under the goal posts.

That was Valkira's cue. *"Ohm . . . . Ohmm . . . . Ohmmm . . . ."*

Suddenly the football team was shivering in their shorts.

There was a shocked silence. Then everyone in the stands was laughing.

The band, meanwhile, was instantly bedecked in smartly-fitting new uniforms, purple trimmed with silver braid. On their tall hats waved thick purple plumes. Mr. Marcheson was stunned to find himself in a handsome white uniform with purple and silver trim.

The band marched proudly out onto the field, sounding as good as it looked. The players carried themselves with impeccable military bearing, executed their complicated maneuvers with perfect precision – and even threw in a few extra difficult moves.

After the performance, the band stood at attention, acknowledging the cheers that went on and on. Mr. Marcheson's face was glowing with pride as he bowed to the thunderous applause.

Valkira closed her eyes and focused. *"Ohm . . . . Ohmm . . . . Ohmmm . . . ."*

And then there she was, in all her purple and silver grandeur. Valkira took a leap of faith, and discovered she could FLY. Which was scary at first – Valkira was glad Grandmère Minerva had insisted on the silver motorcycle helmet. But after a few flights around the field, she discovered that flying – when necessary – was not difficult, especially for a Junior SuperHero.

The band struck up "Stars and Stripes Forever." Mr. Marcheson was amazed that his band not only knew it – but was playing it perfectly. During the piccolo solo, Valkira swooped down and snatched the football from the totally stunned coach. Soaring up, she made several elaborate loops in the air. The football disappeared. Then, as the band played the end of the march, brass blaring triumphantly, Valkira slowly descended with a shiny new sousaphone wrapped around her.

Everyone – especially Mr. Marcheson – cheered wildly, as she presented it to the 1st chair tuba player.

As the band marched triumphantly off the field, Valkira flew proudly overhead. Looking down at the surprisingly skinny football players huddled in their shorts, she flew low and dropped blankets over them. Then Valkira did another big loop and three somersaults for the sheer joy of it.

Ye shall beat thy footballs into sousaphones!

Yes! Justice, at last!

Chapter 4

The System

Valkira brought her oboe along next time she visited Grandmère Minerva. During marching season, she didn't get much chance to play it at school and her embouchure was deteriorating.

"I need to break in some new reeds," she said, putting one to soak in a shot-glass half-filled with water, and the other in a corner of her mouth.

Grandmère Minerva sat down at the harpsichord and flipped through a stack of music on top. "Ah, here it is." She extracted a book of piano exercises, and set it on the music rack. "It's a good day for Bach. You play the right-hand part, and I'll play the rest."

Valkira started slowly with the basic theme, wincing as the new reed squeaked on some of the notes. Then Minerva repeated the theme on the harpsichord. As the variations wove in and out, her body swayed back and forth, her head bobbing on each downbeat. As the tempo increased, oboe and harpsichord chased each other through circles of neatly precise harmony; and when they finally ended on the same chord, grandmother and granddaughter laughed with delight.

"There's nothing like Bach to clear one's head!" exclaimed Minerva with gusto.

"My head needs all it can get of that!" agreed Valkira, setting her oboe carefully across the harpsichord's music rack.

"*Qu'est-ce que c'est?*" asked Katya, sniffing the oboe sarcastically. "*Un canard?*"

"*Non, c'est un hautbois!*" Valkira was offended. "Do I sound that bad?"

"Of course not, dear," Grandmère Minerva said soothingly. "You only sound like a duck when your reed squeaks." She sat down on the divan and lifted Koshka – who was snickering – onto her lap.

Valkira watched Katya carefully, then picked up the cat and sat down on the sofa next to her grandmother. Katya immediately stepped off Valkira's lap, gave herself a hasty bath, then nonchalantly returned.

"A difficult week?" Minerva gave Koshka a warning look. The cat stopped smirking and curled up for a nap.

"A frustrating week! Being a SuperHero isn't as easy as it looks!" Valkira shook her head. "Farts and zits and attack toilets get boring, after awhile.

"Then perhaps you should be more creative."

"But that's not so easy, either," protested Valkira. "I can't sink to their level and just be mean."

"No, of course not," agreed Minerva. "The retribution must be suitable, making the point without injuring."

"The worst is that I keep having to fix the same things over and over!"

"Because people are ignoring you?"

"Oh no! No one ignores <u>me</u> anymore! And no one hassles me – ever! I get lots of respect, and people do – or don't do, as the case may be – whatever I say." Valkira retrieved Katya, who was sniffing the oboe again.

"So what's the problem?"

"Well . . . . things are better for me. And the kids I help don't get picked on as much. But . . . ." Valkira sighed, "nothing really seems to change."

"What should be changing?"

"The whole school!"

"Why?"

"Because it's not a good place for kids to be!"

"And of course you'd like to fix that." Minerva stroked Koshka's fur meditatively. "You'll need help, you know."

"What kind of help? And doing what?"

"In the long run, it's better to help people help themselves, than to keep rescuing them. But it's hard to do that in a bad environment."

"So I need to fix the school?" asked Valkira eagerly. "How?"

"First you need to understand how the system works – and why it doesn't work as well as it should."

"And then?"

"And then empower others to help you fix it!" exclaimed Minerva excitedly, jumping up to get paper-and-pencil.

"*Zut*," mumbled Koshka sleepily, her nap abruptly disturbed.

"We'll need to make a list . . . ."

Ω Ω Ω

Valkira went first to Ms. Anthony.

"What's wrong with this school?" she asked earnestly, pencil and clipboard at the ready.

"Where should I start?!" Ms. Anthony laughed ruefully. "Well – to begin with, there aren't enough good teachers."

"Why not?"

"Because teachers are overworked, underappreciated and underpaid. We are expected to do everything, but get no support from anyone. We have too many kids in our classes, but when we can't 'fix' them, everyone says it's our fault. Worst of all, when we try to help kids who are really messed up, their parents get mad and complain!" Ms. Anthony's face was red and her voice was shaking.

"Then why did you become a teacher?"

"Being a teacher means helping kids learn what they need to know so they can grow up to be responsible people," replied Ms. Anthony. "I'm good at that, and it's what I want to do."

"But you can't do that here?"

"I keep trying," sighed Ms. Anthony. "I love my students and want to help them, but most of the time it's hard to do."

"Do the other teachers feel like you do?"

"Some of them – yes, of course. But most of them have either burned out, become principals, or quit the profession."

"What can I do about it?" asked Valkira, sorry that someone as nice as Ms. Anthony felt so discouraged.

"Just keep being who you are." Ms. Anthony smiled and gave her a hug. "Maybe it'll rub off on the others."

Valkira and her clipboard went next to Mr. Marcheson.

"What's wrong with the school?"

"Well – for openers – Sports are everything," he shook his head ruefully. "And everything else is nothing. Which is sad – tragic, actually – given the world you kids are growing up in. You really need music and art and theatre and such just to keep your sanity."

"I know that." Valkira furrowed her brow. "Why doesn't everyone else?"

"Because people's values are all confused," replied Mr. Marcheson, with genuine concern. "And they don't have their priorities straight."

"What can I do to help?"

"Well," grinned Mr. Marcheson, "that half-time show sure got their attention!" He stood up and saluted her like the drum major.

Next on Valkira's list was Madame Fleur, her French teacher.

"What's wrong with the school?"

"*Mon Dieu,*" groaned Mme Fleur ruefully, "Don't get me started! Well – I'd say it's mainly because people don't understand that we're now part of a global society."

"How does that affect the school?"

"We should be doing everything possible to help our students understand other countries," replied Mme Fleur passionately. "And how better to do that than by studying foreign languages!? But instead, they're being cut from the curriculum!"

"A lot of kids don't think they need to speak another language."

"And here in the USA, probably many of them are right about that." Mme Fleur shrugged. "But that's not why teaching about foreign languages is so important – for us, anyway. How better to crawl inside another culture's head than by seeing how their language works?! It makes one's view of the world bigger! And people more tolerant!"

"*Vive la différence!*"

"Très bien, ma chère," laughed Mme Fleur appreciatively.

"What can I do to help?"

"Well . . . . you certainly set the standard when it comes to being different." Eyebrow arched, Mme Fleur laughed with a nasal French accent. *"Vive la différence!"*

Finally, Valkira – reluctantly – went to see Principal Cox.

"What's wrong with the school?"

He started gearing up to yell, then changed his mind. "We just don't have enough money."

"Then why do you spend so much of it on things that don't matter?"

"Like what?"

"Like football – and sports in general."

Valkira was expecting a coach-like speech about the benefits of teamwork – and so forth, ad nauseam. Instead, Principal Cox hesitated and thought about it.

"I think you underestimate the value of athletic teams," he said finally. "Not all students are smart enough to play in the band, you know."

Valkira was surprised. "Well, OK, maybe so. But why do they get so much more than the band gets?"

"Because that's what the School Board wants."

"But why do they have so much power?"

"Because The Town elects them."

"Oh." Valkira thought about that. "And they do what The Town wants or they won't get re-elected."

"You got it." Principal Cox nodded his head regretfully.

"Do you like being a Principal?" asked Valkira suddenly.

"Not really," he sighed. "I don't especially enjoy being a policeman."

"Do the kids give you a hard time, too?"

"Oh, the kids aren't so bad. It's dealing with their parents that's really tough."

"What can I do to help?"

"Get the parents off my back!" He grinned conspiratorially. "Maybe with something like that stunt you pulled at the football game!"

Leaving his office, Valkira decided that maybe Principal Cox wasn't as bad as she'd thought.

Ω Ω Ω

"What's wrong with the school?" asked Valkira, in between bites of her sandwich.

"That's easy. The kids are too mean to each other!" replied Theodore, who was sitting across from her in the cafeteria.

"But why? Don't they know any better?"

"How could they?" Theodore shook his head ruefully. "Their parents are just as bad."

"Now that you mention it, mine certainly don't set a very good example," agreed Valkira. "Yours, too?"

"All my mother seems to do is buy more stuff – and then worry about how to pay for it."

"Yeah, mine too – but she lets my Dad worry about paying for it."

"All my Dad seems to worry about is why I'm not a jock like he was in school." Theodore frowned. "He'd be really mad if he knew I was in the band – and playing the bassoon, yet!"

"Maybe you should switch to trumpet," grinned Valkira.

"Yeah, maybe," Theodore grinned back. "At least then I wouldn't have to worry about buying new reeds."

"How do you make your reeds last so long?" wondered Valkira. Theodore could keep even the most ancient reeds buzzing far beyond their prime.

"Necessity," grinned Theodore. "My Dad would cut off my allowance if he knew I was spending it on bassoon reeds!"

"If the band got as much money as the football team, you wouldn't have to worry about that."

"That'll be the day!" Theodore took a large bite out of his sandwich and chewed angrily. "The guy next door is on the School Board, and all he ever does is watch football on TV – just like my Dad."

"Yeah, mine too," agreed Valkira sadly. "It's the only time I ever see him without his newspaper. I wish he'd talk to me once in a while."

"I just wish my Dad would stop yelling!" Theodore crumpled up his lunch bag.

"Be glad all he does is yell," said Ophelia, quietly sitting down beside him. "My Dad hits, too. It's why we don't live with him, anymore."

"Is that why you moved here?" asked Valkira, not sure what else to say.

"Yeah, we move a lot. We'll stay here only until he catches up with us again."

"But can't you call the police?

"What good will that do?" Ophelia shrugged sadly. "Mom keeps getting restraining orders, Dad keeps ignoring them, and the police never get there in time."

"But no one should have to live that way!" said Valkira indignantly.

"It's hardest on Mom. She keeps having to change jobs all the time, so we never have enough money. That's why I never tell her about the other girls picking on me."

"I never tell Dad about the bullies, either," said Theodore, who had been listening sympathetically. "He wouldn't hit me – he'd just tell me to 'fight back like a man!' Whatever that means!"

"Maybe it's time I paid a visit to both your fathers!" Valkira's ire was definitely aroused. "In full regalia."

"I've thought about that – many times," grinned Theodore, picturing Valkira's horns zapping his father. "But unless you want to move in with us, I don't think it would stop him for long."

"My Dad, neither," agreed Ophelia, "And you'd have to do something really nasty just to get his attention."

"Then what if <u>you</u> could be SuperHeroes, too?!" exclaimed Valkira excitedly. "You could protect <u>yourselves</u> at home – and at school, you could help me. There's too much to do here for just one SuperHero! And besides, I get lonely always working alone."

"Wow, that would be great!" exclaimed Theodore. "I could make my Dad raise my allowance so I could buy more bassoon reeds!"

"Well, maybe," cautioned Valkira. "But SuperHeroes can't use their power for their own gain – just to protect themselves and help others."

"Not having to play my bassoon with such old reeds would surely protect <u>everyone's</u> ears," grinned Theodore. "And with three of us, we could do a lot more to make this a decent place to be!"

"But how could someone like me be a SuperHero?" Ophelia looked scared.

"I've been wondering about that, too," admitted Theodore.

"Well . . . . First, you have to have a Costume," replied Valkira. "One that says who you really are, and makes you feel strong and brave."

"Where would we get a Costume like that?"

"My grandmother will help you make it!" Valkira was getting really excited. "And she'll show you how to use it."

"When?!"

"Tomorrow, after school," replied Valkira happily. "But tonight, you have to think really hard about who you are and what kind of Costume you need!"

Chapter 5

SuperFriends

Grandmère Minerva was waiting at the door. Dressed in her best chocolate velvet gown, her hair was in a carefully coiffed chignon and the gold spirals danced excitedly from her ears.

"Welcome, welcome!" she smiled, waving Valkira and her friends into the door. Leading them down the hall into the living room, she directed them to the sofa with a great sweeping gesture.

Ophelia and Theodore were speechless. She simply stared, while he tried vainly not to look impressed – but was almost immediately undone by all the books. Floor to ceiling, lining the halls, around the corners, in every room were shelves crammed with more books than he had ever seen – even in the school library.

"Have you read all of these?" asked Theodore, in awe.

"Most of them," replied Grandmère Minerva matter-of-factly. "You're welcome to borrow any of them."

"Oh no, I couldn't . . . . that is, I'd like to . . . . But . . . ." Theodore faltered, " . . . I don't think they would feel at home in my parents' house."

"They're not readers?"

"No," replied Theodore sadly, "Not at all."

"But you have books in your room?"

"Oh, yes!"

"About what?"

"Lots of things!"

"Then I'm sure," smiled Minerva, "that my books would feel at home in your room."

Theodore grinned and sat down on one end of the couch. Koshka, who had been warned beforehand by Minerva, moved over with only a silent *'Zut'*.

Ophelia, meanwhile, was utterly entranced with the musical instruments. "Do you play all of these?"

"Most of them," replied Minerva. "You can come and play them, sometime, if you'd like."

"If only I knew how." Ophelia touched the harpsichord reverently. "We've never lived in one place long enough for me to take lessons."

"Maybe I can help you learn. Mostly it's a matter of encouraging the music in your soul to come out and sing."

Ophelia's face was radiant. It was the first time Valkira had seen her smile. *She's really beautiful when she does that.*

Ophelia sat down on the other end of the sofa. Katya and Koshka immediately curled up next to her, one on either side.

"Bonjour," said Katya cordially.

"Bonjour," echoed Koshka, even more cordially.

"Bonjour," replied Ophelia, petting them both gently. The cats closed their eyes and purred in harmony.

"Wow, they really like you!" remarked Valkira. "You must have a cat."

"I wish I did," answered Ophelia regretfully. "But I've never had a pet."

"Why not?" asked Theodore.

"The landlords never allow it," said Ophelia sadly.

After bringing in a tray of green tea and granola bars, Minerva pulled up a chair facing her guests. "Valkira tells me you need Costumes."

They nodded eagerly.

"Have you decided what kind?"

"I have," said Theodore. "I know exactly what I need."

"Show me." Minerva handed him several sheets of paper and the box of colored pencils.

Theodore immediately began drawing and coloring industriously.

"And what about you?" Minerva turned to Ophelia.

"Well . . . . I'm not sure . . . ."

"How do you want it to make you feel?"

"I don't want to feel scared anymore!"

"And?"

"Well . . . . I'd like to have a wand . . . ." Ophelia hesitated "and I want to wear a crown . . . . and I want to feel beautiful."

"You want to be Homecoming Queen!?!" burst out Valkira in disbelief. "Like Tiffany?!"

"No, no, that's not what I mean!" protested Ophelia. "I don't want to be pretty and popular. I just want people to see me instead of my hand-me-down clothes."

"True Beauty – of any kind – can be very powerful," said Minerva, looking pointedly at her granddaughter. "It can bring out the good in even the worst people."

"Hmm, I never thought of that," said Valkira, hoping she hadn't hurt Ophelia's feelings. "You mean like good music does?"

"Precisely," nodded Minerva approvingly. "Truth and Beauty are just different sides of the same coin. Now let's help Ophelia design a beautiful Costume that will show everyone the Truth of who she is."

After much sketching and coloring, Theodore held up his picture with a flourish. "*Voilà* Owl-Man!" he exclaimed enthusiastically.

"And this is supposed to make you feel smart, right?" guessed Valkira. "But you are smart!"

"Yes, I know," agreed Theodore, "but other people need to know how strong that makes me!"

Ophelia shyly displayed her drawing. Her Costume had lots of flowing veils and flowers and – of course – a crown.

"This should certainly make you look beautiful," said Valkira, still not entirely convinced that something so wispy and fluttery could serve the purpose at hand.

"And if we make it correctly," added Minerva, "It will give you the power of feeling – and being – beautiful."

"Mais oui," concurred Katya and Koshka approvingly.

"Time to go shopping." Swirling on a bright blue velvet cape and donning a matching hat with brown plumes, Minerva led them out the back door. "You three can wait here."

On the porch, next to Valkira's dragon chair were two new chairs; one was shaped like a graceful lyre, the other an abstract owl with feather-like chips. Delighted, Ophelia and Theodore sat down.

"Ярррф! Ярррф! Ярррф!" Olga bounded up to the porch, even more overjoyed than usual, and greeted the guests with effusive hospitality.

"Wow, what a cool dog!" Theodore shook Olga's extended paw. "But why does she bark like that?"

"Because she's a Siberian Husky, of course," answered Ophelia, beaming radiantly at the dog.

When Olga offered her paw to Ophelia, her wildly wagging tail immediately slowed to a gentler pace.

"Ярррф," she sang in a low melodious contralto. "Ярррф."

"I'm happy to meet you, too, Olga," said Ophelia, softly stroking the dog's silver fur and looking directly into her blue eyes. "I'm sorry I don't speak Russian."

"Ярррф," replied Olga, nodding and licking her hand, thinking that the new girl-person spoke dog quite well, albeit with a thick American accent.

When Minerva stepped into Olga's sled, and they flew off over the birch trees, Theodore made no effort to conceal how impressed he was. "Wow! How does she do that!"

"Olga is a SuperHero," said Ophelia. "Obviously."

"Dogs can do that, too?"

"Why not?" shrugged Ophelia.

The three friends sat comfortably on the porch and gazed happily at Minerva's garden – which was presently waving in various hues of blue and green.

"How does she do that?" asked Theodore, indicating the garden of many colors.

"The plants like the music," replied Valkira. "And that Grandmère lets them grow as they please."

"My Mom's garden is in absolutely straight rows," said Theodore. "And she uproots anything that looks like it doesn't belong."

"We've never had a garden," sighed Ophelia. "I think it would be nice to have trees and vegetables and flowers for friends."

The tall prairie grass near the porch – now a nice shade of mauve – leaned toward Ophelia and brushed her cheek gently.

Time passed at its own pace in Minerva's garden. Before Valkira and her friends started wondering when she would return, Olga and the sled flew back over the birch trees and made a flawless landing on the porch. Minerva unloaded several oddly-shaped packages. While she sorted them into two piles, Olga put the sled back in her dacha.

"We'll do Theodore's Costume first," Minerva announced, getting immediately down to business. Unrolling several shades of shiny brown spandex, she measured and cut and sewed the basic garment, fingers flying with their usual speed.

Valkira and her friends, meanwhile, were put to work fastening innumerable feathers onto yards of sturdy yet flexible material.

"Where are the sequins?" wondered Valkira, getting a bit bored with all the feathers.

"Boys don't wear sequins," said Theodore. "Everyone knows that."

"Owls don't wear sequins," corrected Minerva.

When it was finished, Theodore went inside to try it on.

Finally, when Valkira was starting to worry that maybe the toilet had attacked him, Theodore emerged reluctantly from the house, head down and shoulders slumped.

"A SuperHero can't stand like that!" exclaimed Valkira. "You have to walk tall!"

"But . . . . in this?!" As Minerva and the girls regarded his Costume, Theodore was acutely embarrassed.

A long-sleeved unitard of variegated brown stripes covered his entire body. On his feet were brown boots and on his head was a bronze motorcycle helmet with big owl feathers attached. But the *pièce de resistance* of the ensemble was the long feathered cape that opened into a pair of wings.

"What do you mean – 'in this'?!!!" demanded Minerva, who did not take criticism of her creativity well.

"Well . . . . uh . . . . it's the tights . . . ." mumbled Theodore.

"Batman and Superman wear tights!" pointed out Valkira, annoyed that Theodore should be acting like such a typical boy.

"And Spiderman wears a unitard, too," added Ophelia kindly.

"Yes, that's true," conceded Theodore, reconsidering. "And the cape is really cool."

"I think maybe the wings need shortening," said Minerva, kneeling down with pins in her mouth and rapidly hemming the feathered cape. "There! That's better!"

Theodore took another look in the long mirror which had suddenly appeared on the porch. Straightening his shoulders, he tried to look like a SuperHero.

"You need to get into character first," said Minerva, not unkindly. "Close your eyes and think like an owl."

Theodore did as he was told.

"Now talk to me in owl," ordered Minerva.

"In what?!"

"In owl," said Ophelia soothingly. "You know . . . . *Hoo* . . . . *Hooo* . . . *Hoooo* . . . ."

"Hoo . . . . *Hooo* . . . . *Hoooo* . . . ." chanted Theodore. *"Hoo* . . . . *Hooo* . . . . *Hoooo* . . . ."

"Now open your eyes," encouraged Ophelia gently.

Theodore did. And beheld himself transformed. He smiled and spread his wings.

"How do you feel now?" asked Valkira.

"Strong! And brave!" Theodore grinned hugely. "And SMART! Really, really smart!"

"Bravo!" exclaimed Minerva, pleased that Theodore had opted to leave the nest.

"Can I fly with these things?" asked Theodore, flapping his wings.

"When you need to – yes," replied Minerva. "But owls don't flap – they glide."

Theodore continued to gaze raptly at the feathered eminence in the mirror. Olga finally had to tug him away and lead him inside. Carefully, of course, so as not to bruise any of his feathers.

While Theodore was changing, Minerva and the girls started making Ophelia's Costume. Yards of filmy chiffon floated about the porch as Minerva wrapped and arranged and fastened. And Valkira had lots of sequins to sew on. Ophelia, meanwhile, walked in the garden, where flowers of all shapes and colors jumped eagerly into her arms.

"Where is Ophelia's helmet?" wondered Valkira.

"She doesn't need one," replied Minerva. "She won't be doing any flying."

Valkira was relieved. She had been wondering how Ophelia would be able to fly in such a voluminous skirt.

Finally, it was Ophelia's turn to try on her new Costume. When she reappeared, she walked shyly to the mirror.

Ophelia's gown seemed to be made of golden gossamer; its long multi-hued veils floated around her and turned her dull hair into dazzling gold. On her head was a crown of flowers, and in her arms she carried a graceful lyre.

Ophelia stared at the mirror, unable to believe that what she saw could possibly be HER.

"Sing, Ophelia," said Minerva, who had brought her harp out to the porch.

"I don't know how," said Ophelia sadly.

"Yes, you do." Minerva struck a gentle chord. "There's music in your soul just waiting to be set free." Minerva began to play a soft, slow tune.

Ophelia continued to stare at the mirror. Then, unable to resist Minerva's compelling harp, she opened her mouth. Out came the most beautiful song Valkira had ever heard – each note pure and sweet and true.

As Ophelia's voice gained confidence, she began to smile. A warm, golden mist seemed to surround her, and the entire garden began to hum. Olga and the cats sat mesmerized at her feet. And when Ophelia finally believed that the beautiful girl in the mirror was really HER, her song soared forth with Courage and Strength.

As Valkira gazed at Ophelia, tears came to her eyes. Never had she seen anyone so purely lovely and so truly beautiful. Grandmère was right; where Beauty and Truth met was great strength.

Before he went home, Minerva gave Theodore an old slide-rule. "When I was your age, boys like you carried these in their shirt pockets in plastic protectors."

"Like nerd badges?" grinned Theodore.

"That's what the jocks thought – until the 'nerds' used them to make millions." Minerva, too, grinned; she always enjoyed poetic justice. "So use this as a tool to focus your power. Especially when it's not convenient to wear feathers."

"And here is the wand you wanted, Ophelia." Minerva fastened a long silver stick pin in the lapel of her jacket. On top was a small golden lyre. "Use it to help people sing, and they'll forget to pick on you – or anyone else."

"Thank you," said Ophelia with a beatific – and irresistible – smile. "For everything."

"Now, don't forget." Grandmère Minerva hugged them all and opened the front door. "SuperPowers must be used sparingly – and only for good."

"Or else?" grinned Theodore.

"Let's hope you never find out."

Chapter 6

Mass Transformation

Monday morning, Valkira and her friends arrived at school early. Theodore and Ophelia had tried out their new powers on their families. Both were excited about the results.

"Of course, I didn't wear my Costume," said Theodore. "Dad would have freaked out over the feathers! So I just pointed my slide-rule at his remote. Suddenly football became Masterpiece Theatre! Every time he switched back to the game, the TV flipped back to PBS. Finally he gave up and fell asleep."

"How much of Masterpiece Theatre did he actually see?" asked Valkira.

"Probably not too much," grinned Theodore, "But I fixed it so that PBS is the only channel he can get."

"Maybe he'll just stop watching TV."

"And do what?" Theodore chuckled. "Read? Either way, he'll have to think about something besides football."

Valkira made a mental note to try zapping her father's remote.

"Well, I did wear my Costume," said Ophelia. "I just had to let Mom see it. She thought it was beautiful."

"Did you tell her about its power?" asked Valkira, concerned. SuperHeroes were allowed to show – but not tell – these things.

"No, but I <u>had</u> to show her," Ophelia's face was suddenly fearful.

"What happened?" Valkira felt a wave of dread.

"Dad showed up. He'd found us again. Mom told him to stay out, but he barged in anyway. She told me to run – like she always does – and braced herself to get hit."

A vision of her father sitting behind his newspaper flashed before Valkira. *I guess there are worse things than being ignored.*

"But this time, I didn't run away! I started to sing – and suddenly I was in my Costume – and felt so strong and beautiful, I couldn't hate even him."

"What did he do then?"

"He just stared. And dropped his fist." Ophelia was trembling. "And he started to <u>cry</u>!"

"And then?" Valkira put her arm around Ophelia's thin shoulders.

"He finally just walked away."

"And your Mom?"

"For the first time, she didn't look scared. And she said we're NOT going to move again!"

"Hurrah!" shouted Theodore, for once not looking over his shoulder.

Later that day, of course, they caught him.

But Theodore was ready. Whipping out his slide-rule, he took aim and started chanting. *"Hoo . . . . Hooo . . . . Hoooo . . . ."*

The bullies began to jeer. Suddenly, they stopped – mid-guffaw – and were strangely silent. Their eyes glazed over, fixed on the slide-rule.

Slowly Theodore walked down the hall, the pack of bullies trailing him like dogs on a leash. Leading them into the library, he parked each of them at the big table in the far corner.

"Now take out your Algebra books," commanded Theodore.

"Yes, Sir," they answered obediently, fumbling in their backpacks.

"I'm sorry, Sir," said the biggest bully docilely, "but I don't have my book."

"What about your homework?"

"I don't have that, either, Sir."

"I suppose your dog ate it?" asked Theodore sarcastically.

"I don't have a dog, Sir."

Theodore sighed. "You, there," he pointed at the shortest bully, "share your book with the guy who has no sense of humour."

"Yes, Sir," replied the littlest bully, a small smile flitting briefly across his face.

"Now open your books to page 113 and do Problem #9," ordered Theodore.

The boys looked at him blankly."

"Well, what's the problem?" Theodore frowned, wondering if his slide-rule had run out of steam.

"The problem, Sir," answered the least unintelligent bully, "is that we don't know how to do the Problem."

"Well, then," replied Theodore, relieved, "Pay attention, and I'll show you how."

And they did.

A few of them got it right away; others needed further explanation. One by one, Theodore saw them smile as they realized that they <u>could</u> do this. When the bell rang, only the biggest bully hadn't figured out the problem.

Ophelia, meanwhile, had been busy, too. In the locker room before Gym class, the girls with big chests started their usual harassment. Ophelia closed her eyes. *"Do . . . . Re . . . . Mi . . . . Dooo . . . . Reee . . . . Miii . . . ."* And suddenly she was standing on the locker room bench, chiffon veils flowing and golden hair dazzling.

A gasp swept the locker room as all the girls clustered around Ophelia on her pedestal, and gazed at her stunning Costume. Before admiration could turn to envy, Ophelia began to sing, slowly turning and pointing her lyre at the heart of each girl in the circle gathered around her. Ophelia's song was soft and gentle and sweet, and soon the girls were singing with her, amazed at how lovely all their voices sounded together.

When it was over, they were silent. And then walked slowly and peacefully out of the locker room. Ophelia was once again in her hand-me-downs, but no one noticed. And no one bothered her.

The next day in Algebra class, Theodore pointed his slide-rule at the brightest bully, who 'volunteered' to do a problem on the board. To everyone's amazement – especially his own – he did it correctly. He smiled, confused by the pleasant sensation of having used his mind and gotten it right. On the way back to his seat, he glanced suspiciously at Theodore.

After school, they caught him again, and he again diverted them to the library and ordered them to do their homework. This time, more of them got it sooner, and the next day the brightest bully volunteered to do a problem without prodding by Theodore's slide-rule.

And so it went, all week. Each day, Mr. Quark was more amazed at how well his worst students were doing. Finally, in the library on Friday, Theodore *Hoo-Hoooo-Hoooo*ted all his feathers on and addressed the erstwhile bullies in full owl regalia.

"OK! Now you know how to do the Problems, right?" Theodore spread his wings majestically.

The fledgling mathematicians nodded, impressed – and more than a little apprehensive.

"You know how to use your minds," Theodore continued, giving his wings a few trial flaps. "It feels good, doesn't it?!"

They nodded, wondering what he would do next.

"DOESN'T IT!?!"

"YES, SIR!!!"

"And now you're going to do your homework and pass all the tests – ON YOUR OWN!"

"But, Sir," said the littlest bully, "we can't do it by ourselves."

"Then help each other," said Theodore, jumping up on the library table. "And ask Mr. Quark for help – that's what teachers are for."

And then Theodore spread his wings wide, in what he hoped was proper gliding form, and took a leap of faith. He soared into the air, circled the room twice, then glided out the window.

Never again was anyone's head flushed in the toilet at Jane Addams Junior High School.

Ophelia, meanwhile, began to stay after school, usually in Mrs. Price's chorus room. Some of the other girls began to follow her there, at first hoping to see for themselves the locker room transformation everyone was talking about. Ophelia, however, realized the wisdom of Minerva's advice not to overuse her Costume.

Instead, she sang. And the girls began to sing with her. And stopped caring about what she was wearing – and what they were wearing. And started to remember how being kind felt, and how good it was to be with someone who was without meanness. Ophelia's choir grew steadily; eventually even the cheerleaders joined. None of them ever spoke to Ophelia anywhere else. But in that room, after school, everyone felt beautiful and safe.

Ω Ω Ω

As the semester progressed, Valkira began to sense a qualitative change in the atmosphere at school. The jocks strutted less, snotty swishing of cheerleader skirts decreased, bullying virtually disappeared. Cliques, of course, remained – but without overt inter-group hostility. Overall, Jane Addams Junior High was a kinder, gentler place these days.

Which made it easier for students to concentrate on what was, after all, the school's main purpose. As more and more students began to actually study, even some of the burned-out teachers came to life and remembered the thrill of helping kids learn. Student behavior improved, and rarely was anyone sent to the Principal's office. Classes became more interesting and grades went up. Valkira was no longer the only member of the academic team answering questions.

Best of all, the tyranny of adolescent conformity began to fade. Being different was no longer anathema, sameness not a requirement for survival. Individualism began to cautiously peek out of the cocoon of puberty. Valkira herself became something of an icon among those hardy souls who sought more creative personae. Though she rarely wore her Costume, her school clothes developed a distinctive style that she wore with panache. (Always, of course, within bounds of the dress code.) Other students followed suit, each in their own way.

"I think we should celebrate!" Valkira and her friends were in the band room, where they often hung out. "Not just us, but everyone in the whole school!"

"I agree." Theodore fiddled with the feather quill he usually wore behind his left ear. "But not a prom or a pep rally or – horrors! – a football game."

"Why not just have a half-time show," smiled Ophelia, "and forget about the game."

"That's a good idea," said Valkira, glad that Ophelia was smiling so much lately. "But I think we'd need to enlarge the whole concept of half-time."

"To more than marching, you mean." Theodore put the feather back behind his ear. "And probably more than just band music, too."

"Maybe we could do something that would involve everyone – even the jocks."

"Like a circus?" suggested Ophelia.

"Sort of. But not a regular circus. The idea would be to get everyone to do something they really enjoy."

"And they could wear Costumes that show who they really are," added Ophelia, her smile bigger and more beautiful than ever, "like ours do."

Valkira and her friends got busy and started organizing. Many of the teachers, too, were enthused and offered to sponsor the event. Principal Cox even gave permission to use the Gymnasium.

By unanimous consent, Valkira, Theodore and Ophelia became the Advisory Committee, whose job was to help the other students decide what to do and wear. They sat at a long table in Ms. Anthony's room, and interviewed the students one by one. Theodore aimed his slide-rule at their heads; Ophelia pointed her lyre at their hearts. Valkira wore her purple horned helmet as a symbol of her own unique identity.

The students who presented themselves consequently thought hard about who they really were. The presence of the school's most notorious nonconformist inspired them to want to be that real self. And the aura of gentle kindness that pervaded any room Ophelia was in made them feel safe enough to drop their masks.

As it turned out, the students of Jane Addams Junior High were a very creative and interesting group. And extremely – and delightfully – diverse. It was going to be a <u>wonderful</u> Celebration!

Some of them, of course, were rather predictable. Ashley, for example, wanted to be a ballet dancer. "I want to move with grace and elegance," she said passionately, "not just shake my fanny!" The Committee advised her to study Russian Ballet.

Tracey wanted to be a Mermaid and do Synchronized Swimming. The Committee directed her to watch old Esther Williams movies.

The biggest bully – to no one's surprise – wanted to be a clown. The Committee pointed him toward the legendary clowns of Barnum & Bailey, and the Moscow Circus.

Theodore was especially proud when Albert, the brightest of his former bullies, stated that he wanted to be a rocket scientist.

The Committee turned him loose with books on stage design and videotapes of the Cirque du Soleil.

The real surprises began when Eugene, the littlest ex-bully, confessed his love for figure-skating. "The way those guys go whizzing across the ice and do those incredible jumps is fantastic. But the best thing" – he hesitated and looked at Ophelia for encouragement – "is how beautiful they look when they just glide. That must feel wonderful."

The Committee suggested he watch Figure-Skating Competitions on TV.

"I already do – late at night, of course. Once my older brother walked in on me," Eugene grinned sheepishly. "I told him I was just watching the little skirts on the girl-skaters."

Stacey was next. "I am so sick of people always staring at my boobs! Sometimes I just want to smack some of the boys! Why can't anyone take me seriously as a person?!"

The Committee advised her to watch re-runs of "Xena, Warrior Princess" and to find some "Wonder Woman" comic books.

Louie the Quarterback, who – after one look at Ophelia – admitted that his real name was Ludwig, confided his passion for classical music. The Committee urged him to practice more for his secret piano lessons, and to listen to all of Beethoven's symphonies.

The biggest surprise, however, was Elijah, captain of the football team. "Listen, man, if it were up to me, I'd get rid of football. All those pads and stuff are too heavy for kids our age – and even the older guys are always ruining their knees."

"Then why not just quit?" asked Valkira.

"That's easy for you to say," replied Elijah. "You're really smart and can get scholarships to places like Harvard. For guys like me, athletics is the best ladder up."

"But you're not stupid," objected Theodore.

"I know that. But Sports is what I do best."

"Then what's the problem?" wondered Ophelia.

"It's not FUN anymore! That's what playing games is supposed to be about, right? All my Dad – and the other Dads – care about is winning. I wish they'd <u>all</u> stay home!!"

"Then why not make up a new game?!" exclaimed Valkira. "One that <u>is</u> fun – and everyone can play – and no one gets hurt. And winning doesn't matter!"

Elijah's face lit up. As he left the room, the wheels of his mind were racing madly.

Ω Ω Ω

By the day of the big event, the entire school was totally involved. Since helping students discover who they are, what they do best, and how to do it with others, was – after all – the main purpose of the school, all of the classes focused on preparation. Principal Cox even announced that the Celebration would take the place of Final Examinations.

The teachers decided that they, too, would wear Costumes. Ms. Anthony, of course, was dressed as a suffragette, carrying a sign that proclaimed "Equal Pay for Equal Work - Ratify the ERA!" Mr. Quark appeared as Mr. Spock, wearing pointed ears and greeting everyone with the "Live Long and Prosper" salute. Mr. Marcheson showed up as Fred Astaire, tap shoes flashing with debonair rhythm. His top-hat and tails looked especially dapper next to the dark raincoat and weathered fedora worn by Principal Cox, who came as Vince Lombardi. 'Diva' Price looked very Egyptian as Aida, and frequently broke into fulsome operatic song. And Mme Fleur was stylishly statuesque as the Statue of Liberty.

"Well, after all, she was made in France," she sniffed, lifting her torch proudly.

Mrs. Stewart and her cooking class wore chef hats and offered trays of sushi and escargots to the assembled participants. C.Chaplin – as the biggest former bully now called himself – was wearing orange hair, a big red nose, a little black mustache and baggy black pants. He was picking flowers out of everyone's ears, trailed by a trio of jugglers riding unicycles.

The program opened with Ashley and her corps de ballet doing a scene from "Swan Lake". Half of their feathers were crooked, and some of the back-up dancers looked rather lumpish in their tutus, but Ashley herself danced so ecstatically that no one noticed. Ophelia shouted "Brava!" and presented her with a bouquet. Ashley bowed graciously, then ran *en pointe* off the stage, clad in the Costume Ophelia and her mother had helped her make.

Suddenly the stage became a swimming pool, with Tracey – dressed as a mermaid – on the diving board. She was flanked by a line of more mermaids, poised on the racing platforms. One by one, they jumped into the pool and formed a circle, into which Tracey dove, straight as an arrow. With the Beach Boys singing "Surfin' USA," the swimmers performed an intricate series of rhythmic kicks and plunges. In the grand finale, their mermaid tails formed a giant surfboard, on which Tracey caught a wave, balancing precariously on her fins. Then the lights went out.

When the lights came on again, the water in the swimming pool had turned to ice. Eugene whizzed out onto the rink, tried to spin and tripped on his blades. But instead of jeering, everyone shouted words of encouragement. Eugene stood up, grinned, and attempted a very elementary single jump. He landed, wobbling, then straightened and held up both arms victoriously. Everyone cheered.

Then out skated Hortense, the tallest girl at Jane Addams Junior High. And the homeliest. <u>Everyone</u> thought so – even Valkira. But Ophelia's Mom had helped Hortense, too, with her Costume. She looked better than anyone had ever seen her.

As the opening strains of a Strauss Waltz sounded, Eugene skated up to Hortense, bowed low and held out his hand. She gracefully placed her hand in his, and they began to glide around the ice. As the music picked up the waltz tempo, their skates flashed in rhythm and their bodies leaned as one. And as the circles they inscribed together grew bigger and happier, short-and-tall became irrelevant. All anyone could see was the beauty of their joyous movement.

Afterward, it took a long time to gather all the flowers which rained on the ice.

Then a large mat covered the ice rink. Stacey ran out, clad in blue tights and a red T-shirt with a gold eagle emblazoned on the front. With the aid of the wrestling team, she proceeded to give a demonstration of self-defense techniques. First the ersatz muggers attempted to subdue her with various oddly-shaped projectiles, which she deftly repelled with the thick metal bracelets on her wrists. They then charged her en masse. Ululating raucously, Stacey spun in a circle, fending off each of them with a series of flashing kicks. Finally, the wrestlers all fell in a heap. Stacey placed one foot on the pile and, raising her arms triumphantly, gave a final victorious whoop. All the girls – and most of the smaller boys – cheered wildly.

Behind the scenes, Albert was masterminding all of the dramatic set changes. And enjoying it so much that designing rockets seemed to him rather pedestrian by comparison. He flipped several switches, and suddenly the mat rolled back and the ice rink became a giant trampoline, with several hoops suspended above and a big platform in each corner.

Elijah jumped off one of the platforms, bounced up into a somersault and landed in the center of the court. "This is a new game, and we're going to show you how it's played." Elijah waved to the other athletes on the platforms. "You get one point for throwing a ball through a hoop, another point if someone on the other team catches it, and two points if you jump through a hoop yourself and somebody catches you." Elijah and the other players were dressed in padded jumpsuits and lightweight helmets. "And the object of the game is to play to a draw."

Principal Cox, in his Vince Lombardi coat and hat, scowled. Nevertheless, he blew his referee's whistle.

Soon the air was filled with flying bodies and zooming balls. At first, there was the usual blocking and intercepting and teams competing. Gradually, however, the players began to realize that business-as-usual wouldn't do the job. Opposing teams began to cooperate in order to score points. And discovered that evening the score was not as easy as it sounded.

When Principal Cox-Lombardi blew the final whistle, he was no longer scowling.

Up in the control booth, Albert flipped one last switch. The trampoline turned into a huge stage big enough for the whole school.

The band was sitting in concert formation, surrounded on three sides by a large chorus of almost everyone else. Ludwig, as he now insisted everyone call him, walked out and stepped onto the podium. He was followed by Ophelia in her glorious golden Costume.

Ludwig had composed an original cantata for the Finale. He raised his baton, gave the downbeat, and the band began to play. Then Ophelia started to sing, and the entire chorus joined in. Never had Valkira heard such beautiful music. Never had she felt so connected to people with whom she had thought she could never belong.

Tonight there was no need to chant. After carefully putting her oboe on her chair, she flew up into the air, sequined cape flapping and purple horns shooting sparks. Theodore laid down his bassoon, exploded into feathers, and zoomed up to join Valkira.

As Ludwig's music reached its triumphant climax, Valkira and Theodore soared and swooped around Ophelia. She opened her arms – and suddenly the whole world was in tune.

Part II

Omega

Chapter 7

Money

"THEY'RE GOING to fire our best teachers!" Valkira burst angrily into Grandmère Minerva's house.

"What?!" Minerva was alarmed. "Who?!"

"Mr. Marcheson and Mrs. Price – and Mme Fleur." Valkira was fuming. "And even Ms. Anthony."

"So they're dropping Music and Foreign Language from the curriculum. What fools!" Minerva, too, was irate. "But why Ms. Anthony? Surely they aren't cutting History, too?!"

"Supposedly it's because she has less seniority," replied Valkira, disgusted. "But I think it's because she's a feminist!"

"So who will teach History?"

"Boring old Mr. Stamps, who just drones on and on about dates and battles and stuff. That's not History!"

"I don't suppose funding for any of the athletic teams is being cut?"

"Of course not!" Valkira was close to tears. "And the School Board warned Principal Cox that there are to be no more Celebrations. And they want him to confiscate our Costumes."

"Is he going to follow orders!"

"Not entirely. Even he knows how much better the school is now. He said he won't take our Costumes or forbid what we do, but we have to keep a low profile."

"I wonder why the School Board is banning the Celebrations. Everyone in town thought the first one was wonderful."

"Principal Cox said they were afraid we wouldn't score high enough on the standardized tests, and that then the school wouldn't get funding from the government."

"Money! Again! Why is there never enough for the important things!" Minerva began to pace angrily.

"Why does Money matter so much?" asked Valkira, perplexed.

Minerva stopped pacing and stared at Valkira. Going to her purse, she pulled out a dollar bill and looked thoughtfully at it. "Yes . . . . why should this have so much power?"

"It's just a piece of paper."

"But it represents something much more powerful."

"But how?" asked Valkira urgently, knowing she had put her finger on something very important. "And why?"

"I can't answer that," replied Minerva, "but I know who can! Your father!"

"Dad?!"

"Of course! He works at a big bank in The City! He knows about these things."

"Dad?!"

"Of course! Why do you think he's always reading the *Wall Street Journal*?"

"I thought it was to hide from us."

"Well – that, too," agreed Minerva, frowning. "But it's time he put down his paper and started telling you what he does all day."

"Dad?! But he never talks about anything – except once in a while about football with Brad."

"Maybe you should ask him about something else."

Later, after dinner, Valkira tried. Harold was sitting in His Chair, behind his newspaper as usual.

Valkira sat down in the chair next to him. "Um, Dad," she cleared her throat nervously, "what is Money?"

The newspaper was suddenly very still. "What kind of question is that?" said the unfamiliar voice behind the paper after a long silence.

"What is Money?" Valkira repeated. "Why is it so powerful?"

Harold finally put down the *Wall Street Journal.* "Because it's – MONEY. And it's very valuable."

"But it's just a piece of paper."

"No – it's a very special kind of paper."

"But why is this one," Valkira fumbled in her pocket, and then held up a one dollar bill next to a piece of 'Monopoly' money, "worth more than this one?"

"Because the government says so."

"Why?"

"Because it's easier to carry around money, than for everyone to trade each other for what they need."

"But doesn't that make it easier for some to get more than they need?"

"Not necessarily," replied Harold rather smugly. "But it's certainly easier for those of us wise enough to accumulate it."

"Do you have a lot of money?"

"Well – yes – more than most."

"More than Ophelia's Mom?"

"Well – yes – probably."

"Why?"

"Well – I have a job and get paid to do it."

"Ophelia's Mom has two jobs."

"Well . . . . I work very hard."

"So does Ophelia's Mom. She's too tired to sit and read the newspaper when she gets home from work!"

"Well . . . . It's complicated."

"Then explain it to me."

"The system is too complex to explain!" Harold was getting irritated.

"Then show it to me," Valkira persisted, "like you did when you took Brad to work with you last year."

"But that was Father-Son Day at the bank."

"Don't they have a Father-Daughter day, too?"

"No, of course not."

"Why not?"

"Because they just don't!" Harold put his *Wall Street Journal* back up and said no more.

When Valkira told her grandmother about the conversation, Minerva was furious. REALLY furious! "Hmmmph! We'll just see about that!!!"

Minerva showed up, unannounced, after dinner the next evening, clad in her darkest brown cloak and most formidable hat. Millicent, who was terrified of her mother-in-law, opened the door and blanched.

Minerva, who considered her daughter-in-law incredibly shallow and impossibly frivolous, nodded curtly and swept passed her to the 'Family Room'. Harold was in His Chair and behind his newspaper, as usual, waiting for the football game to start. Cape swirling majestically, Minerva imperiously raised her arm, zapping the remote and the *Wall Street Journal* simultaneously. Standing in front of the TV screen, she glared down at her son.

"Hello, Mother," mumbled Harold, looking even more terrified than Millicent, who had retreated to the kitchen.

"Why don't you ever talk to your daughter!?!" demanded Minerva, getting right to the point.

"Which one?" Harold tried to temporize – and immediately regretted it.

"You know very well!!!" Minerva's anger escalated several notches. "The one you haven't let your feather-brained wife ruin yet!!!"

"I don't know what to say to her," replied Harold miserably, sweating profusely under his mother's irate gaze.

"Try answering her questions, for starters!"

"What questions?" Harold was a terrible liar.

Minerva glared at him.

"Oh, those questions." Harold squirmed in his chair. "It's too complicated for her to understand."

"That's absurd!" snorted Minerva. "If Bradford can get it, anyone can!"

"But Valkira's too young."

"Bah! You're just worried that she'll ask embarrassing questions!"

Harold hung his head miserably.

"Either you take Valkira to work with you, or I will!" Minerva's smile was chilling. "Then you can show us both around that bank of yours."

Looking as though he might faint, Harold acquiesced.

Ω Ω Ω

On Tuesday of the following week, Valkira boarded the commuter train with her father and brother. Harold had decided to bring Bradford along, for protection. Father and son chatted briefly about the most recent football game; Harold then retreated behind his newspaper and Brad dozed off. Everyone else on the train seemed to be reading the *Wall Street Journal*, too. Valkira liked trains, and eagerly watched the houses and fields and trees whiz by her window.

As they pulled into the train station, everyone folded their newspapers, put them in their briefcases, and lined up at the door.

On the platform, Valkira followed the hurrying crowd, almost running to keep up with the long strides of Dad and Brad. For a moment, she was tempted to *Ohm*, but decided that her father would be mortified by the purple horns. It would be best not to make his mood worse than it already was.

The Bank where Harold worked was on the main street of The City. It was big and imposing, with huge stone columns guarding its heavy bronze doors. The large room inside had high ceilings and marble floors. Their footsteps echoed as they walked past the gold cages lining the walls.

"What are these?" asked Valkira, lowering her voice in the almost quiet room.

"That's where the tellers give people money," replied Harold, in a voice at least as reverent as the one he used in church.

"Can anyone just ask for it?"

"No, of course not, silly," laughed Brad, who had stuck his hands in his pockets in lieu of having a ball to carry. "You've got to have an account."

"I know that," replied Valkira, irritated. "I was asking how you get an account in the first place."

"You would ask to open an account," said Harold, addressing his daughter directly for the first time since they had boarded the train.

"Can I do that now?"

"Do you have any money?"

"No – why would I need an account if I already had money?"

"Because it's safer to leave it here than to carry it around."

"What does The Bank do with it?"

"The Bank gives it to people who need to buy homes and businesses – things like that."

"Ophelia and her mother would like to move out of their little apartment. Could she borrow money here to buy a house?" Valkira asked, excited.

"No, I'm afraid not." Harold's tone was patronizing. "I doubt that her credit rating would be sufficient. We can't lend money to people who don't have enough to pay it back."

"But if they can afford to pay it back, why would they need to borrow in the first place?" persisted Valkira.

Dad and Brad rolled their eyes *à deux*. Valkira decided to drop it and move on.

"OK, so let's say I have some money and open an account here so it will be safe. Then you give it to someone else. What's in it for The Bank?"

"We charge interest," replied Harold, relieved that the conversation was back on a comfortable track.

"And what's in it for me?"

"You get some of that interest, too." Harold smiled, thinking that his daughter was finally catching on.

"So I get money, even though I don't work for it? That doesn't seem fair."

Harold sighed, and quickened his pace. At the other end of the room full of tellers' cages was the door to his department. In big gold letters was a sign that said '**INVESTMENTS**'. Harold's office was one of the bigger cubicles. He sat down in the ergonomic chair behind the big desk, and directed his children to the two chairs on the other side. On the desk was a large photograph of Millicent and Tiffany – both smiling toothily – in a mother-daughter cheerleading pose. The skirt of Millicent's vintage outfit was considerably longer than Tiffany's, but it still fit quite well. Next to them was an even bigger photo of Bradford in his football uniform, his usual grin overlaid by something that was supposed to look aggressive. Other than the pictures, nothing in her father's office relieved its institutional uniformity. A vision of Grandmère Minerva's crowded house flashed before Valkira. And for the millionth time, she wondered how such a mother could have spawned such a son.

"What, exactly, do you do here?" asked Valkira, getting directly to the main point of the excursion.

"He helps people make money," answered Brad, showing off.

"You mean they print a batch themselves?! I thought only the government could do that."

Brad sighed, and handed off the question to his father.

"No, no, we don't literally print money. We increase the amount credited to someone's account."

"How?"

"By advising them to invest money in stocks and bonds that pay dividends."

"Is that like interest?"

"Almost, but it's paid by the company that's using your money instead of by The Bank."

"So, again, people get money without doing any work?"

"Well, yes, but only if the stock goes up in value."

"And who decides that?"

"The Market."

"And who runs that?"

"Well, no one actually. It's just a term we use to describe the Law of Supply and Demand."

"Who made this Law? Congress?"

"No one made it. It just exists."

"What if The Market doesn't work?"

"Then just leave it alone, and it will fix itself."

"If it doesn't, do people get their money back?"

"No."

"So it's sort of like gambling."

Harold was silent. Valkira deemed it prudent to pursue a different line of questioning.

"So if I had money, what kind of stock would you advise me to invest in."

"Stock issued by companies that make money."

"But what if they sell stuff that's bad for people?"

"Then people shouldn't buy it."

"And if they do?"

"That's not The Market's fault," shrugged Harold. "A business just gives people what they want to buy."

Valkira was about to argue, then decided against it. There was still one more thing she needed to understand.

"So – let's see if I have this right – the more money someone has, the more they can get?"

"That's correct."

"And people with lots of money are more powerful than people who don't have much."

"Usually, yes."

"Does that mean rich people are better than poor people?"

"Well, most poor people are poor because they're lazy and don't want to work."

"But rich people get interest and dividends – so they don't work, either."

Harold abruptly decided it was time to go to lunch. They went to The Club. It was, he explained proudly, the best club in The City.

The Club wasn't as big as The Bank, but loudly proclaimed 'Old Money'. Inside, it smelled of expensive leather and Cuban cigars. There was a tastefully muscular doorman in an elegant uniform guarding the inner entrance. He greeted Harold deferentially, and Bradford somewhat less so, but still cordially.

And then he saw Valkira. And almost panicked when she started walking in the door.

"Oh but, Sir, you know we don't allow any – ah – children in The Club."

Never having attempted to bring any – ah – children to The Club before, Harold was nonplused.

"But maybe the – ah – child could wait in the kitchen – I'm sure the cooks could find some nice treats – while you have lunch." The doorman was struggling not to violate the cardinal rule of never embarrassing a Club Member. He made a quick phone call, while Dad and Brad fidgeted – and Valkira tried to decide whether or not to *Ohm*.

Before she had made up her mind, a small Asian man in a waiter's uniform appeared and led her to the servants' entrance.

The kitchen was filled with people of almost all ages, genders and races, but she was the only WASP in the room. A large African-American woman sat her down at a table in a corner, and proceeded to load her plate with all kinds of interesting food.

"It's all right, Honey," she said with a friendly grin, "We eat better back here, anyway."

After several helpings of truly delectable entrées and a couple of obscenely delicious desserts, Valkira was inclined to agree.

Even so, she was angry. She knew very well that Bradford had never been denied access to the main entrance when he was – ah – a child.

Grandmère Minerva would definitely hear about this!

And then, heaven help her father!

Chapter 8

The Club

Minerva was sitting on her back porch, deep in thought. She was angry – thoroughly and righteously so. The cats were under a chair on the other end of the porch, pretending to sleep, eyeing her nervously through barely opened lids. The trees were silent and grey; the flowers had closed their blossoms. Even Olga was sitting cautiously in her dacha, waiting for Minerva's heavy mood to lift.

The target of her wrath was multiple.

First, there was the school. Just when Jane Addams Junior High was actually becoming a real school, the School Board was pulling the plug! What idiots! Valkira and her friends had worked so hard, and done so much – more than children should have to do. And the adults had let them down. Again.

And then there was her son. How could he treat his own daughter as if she didn't exist? How could he regard being the father of such a wonderful child as a nuisance?! Why was he such a fool?!

Valkira had given her a thorough report about her excursion to The City. The incident at The Club rankled. But what had enraged Minerva was what her granddaughter had learned about MONEY: It was powerful. It was unfairly distributed. It was without conscience or morality. It did not reward merit or hard work. And – most mind-boggling of all – it did not really exist – except in the minds of those who manipulated it.

But everyone seemed to accept all of this without question. Even she herself had – until now. Which was why she was angry at herself, too. It wasn't enough to enlighten and encourage and make granola bars. She also had to understand what threatened her granddaughter's well-being. *And I have to DO something about it!*

Minerva went inside, to the desk in her study. In the bottom drawer – which she rarely opened – was a thick stack of financial statements that were regularly forwarded by her son's office. They were written in complicated jargon, which Minerva had always assumed she didn't need to understand. Taking a closer look, however, she realized that what the various reports actually said was much simpler than it appeared to be. But it was also intensely boring.

She sat down at her desk and started reading and sorting – which felt like trying to tie knots out of fog. Several times she almost dozed off; only her outrage kept her plowing through the greyness emanating from the documents.

By morning, she had finished. Yawning, she threw most of the papers away, and put the relevant ones in a gold attaché case. Returning to the porch, she announced to all that she was ready to do what needed to be done, and that they could all quit hiding.

"*Quelle relève!*" exclaimed Katya and Koshka.

"Ярррф! Ярррф!" barked Olga happily.

The trees and flowers gave an audible sigh of relief, and resumed their waving and color-changing.

Minerva went back inside, and dressed carefully. From the back of her closet, she pulled out a russet-red velvet gown she hadn't worn in years. It still fit, though was styled more elaborately than her usual plain browns. Over it she draped a burgundy-colored cloak, and put on the matching hat. It showed off her chignon nicely and gave the impression of being a crown. Checking her reflection in the mirror, she touched the pendant around her neck; the sapphire turned into a large ruby, and the gold spirals hanging from her ears grew longer.

"Ярррф!" Olga and the sled were waiting on the porch. Red ribbons fluttered from her harness, and her tail wagged with extra enthusiasm. "Ярррф! Ярррф!"

Minerva stepped carefully into the sled and sat down among the furs. Olga took off and flew over the birch trees toward The City. Minerva liked flying, and usually enjoyed watching the houses and fields whiz by underneath the sled. Today, however, she was preoccupied, thinking about how best to make her case.

Olga made a flawless landing right in front of The Club.

The tastefully muscular doorman stared, then made a quick recovery. "Um . . . . That's a No Parking zone."

"ГрррЛ . . . ." Olga bared her teeth and sat down on the sidewalk.

Minerva alighted gracefully and headed purposefully for the door.

"I'm sorry," said the doorman, rushing back to the entrance, "but this is a Private Club."

"Yes, I know," Minerva said sweetly. "My son is a member, and I am his guest."

"But – ah – we don't allow – ah . . . ."

"Yes, I know, you don't allow – ah – children." Minerva smiled brightly. "Well, I'm certainly not one of THOSE!" And with that, she swept regally through the door.

Inside was a huge room, filled with overstuffed leather chairs. In each chair was a man of somewhere around middle-age, puffing a long cigar and reading the *Wall Street Journal*. On the table at his elbow was a glass of expensive Scotch, neat.

Minerva spotted Harold at the far end of the room – he had a very distinctive tilt to his newspaper that she recognized at once. She strode fearlessly through the avenue of chairs; in her wake followed spilled Scotch, breaking glass, gasps of horror – even cardiac arrest. The smell of burning paper indicated that

Cuban cigars and the *Wall Street Journal* had inadvertently made contact.

Minerva pointed imperiously at an empty chair in the corner, which immediately appeared opposite Harold. "We need to talk," she said, sitting down and putting her gold attaché case on her lap.

"Mother . . . ." gasped Harold, horrified. "You – you shouldn't . . . b-b-be here!"

"Don't worry, dear," replied Minerva, snapping open her case, "I'm not one of those – ah – children, so it's all right."

"What do you want?" asked Harold, his face purple with mortification.

"I want you to make some changes in my stock portfolio." Minerva pulled out a list and handed it to him.

"But Mother," he protested weakly, "you've always let me manage these things for you."

"Things change," she replied curtly, "when they need to."

As Harold carefully scanned the list, his face turned from purple to white. "This says to sell all but one share of each of the blue-chip stocks – and then to invest what's left in these companies I've never even heard of!"

"That's because they are Socially Responsible businesses who try to help people and repair the Environment – instead of just ripping it off!"

"But Mother, you won't make very much money with these!"

"Will I make enough?"

"Well, yes, but . . . ."

"Then do it! Enough is Enough!" Minerva closed her attaché case and stood up. Striding back through the wreckage of broken glass and burning newspaper, she flung back over her shoulder, "Because if you don't, I shall return!"

"Noooooooo . . . ." A mighty gasp of horror arose, in unison, from the overstuffed chairs.

Ω Ω Ω

Minerva exited The Club feeling much better than when she had entered. The doorman was cowering near the entrance. Olga was still sitting on the sidewalk, giving him baleful looks and occasionally growling. A policeman had given her a parking ticket, which she had defiantly eaten. A few leftover pieces were scattered disdainfully on the ground.

Minerva stepped regally into the sled and remained standing. With an imperious sweep of her cape, she signaled Olga to take off – very carefully. Traffic stopped as dog and sled flew into the air, Minerva at the helm like Washington crossing the Delaware. Once out of sight, she sat down and told Olga to go to The Sanctuary.

The Sanctuary was on the edge of The City. In its prime it had been a popular amusement park, but had since been left behind by modern entertainment technology. As Olga circled for a landing, Minerva noted that the parking lot of the old castle was filled with familiar conveyances.

Olga pulled in next to a Troika, whose horses shook their bells in welcome and neighed excitedly in Russian. "Ярρрф!" Olga was happy to see her friends. On the other side was a sleepy-looking burro, who was not especially fond of the noisy Russians, who – in turn – usually ignored her. Beside the burro was a Roman chariot; between its traces sat an old camel, placidly chewing her cud. Parked next to the chariot, was a very small Japanese hybrid car. And further down the line was tethered a hot-air balloon decorated with avant-garde designs.

Minerva entered the main room of the castle, which had been converted into a coffeehouse. Banners inscribed in numerous languages hung around its circular walls. Music blending the best of several cultures echoed from the high ceiling. Sitting around tables painted with various exotic designs were dozens of grandmothers, all dressed in distinctively different, colorfully ethnic Costumes.

Greeting several of the women, Minerva made her way through the humming kaleidoscope of tongues to a table near the center.

"*Hola!*" Maria waved animatedly and greeted her warmly.

"*Bonjour!*" Simone displayed her most Gallic grin.

Shizuka bowed and smiled.

"*Buongiorno! Buongiorno!*" Sophia's hands gestured excitedly at the empty chair next to her. "*Prego, Prego!*"

Babushka Ekaterina enveloped her in a firm hug.

Minerva sat down next to Sophia, and unfastened her cloak. They had all been friends for years. And though each woman spoke her native language, she was understood by the others with no need of translation.

"We have missed you, Minerva," said Babushka Ekaterina, in a deep voice that sounded a lot like Olga's.

"My Work has been very time consuming lately," replied Minerva, taking a sip of the latte that appeared on the table.

"*Mais oui,*" said Simone with measured sympathy. "Young Valkira is coming of age, *n'est-ce pas?*"

"It is a difficult time," observed Maria volubly.

"But a glorious time!" Sophia's hands were eloquent. "Full of the romance and drama of youth!"

"Which requires much subtlety," added Shizuka quietly.

"And I think it's becoming harder than ever," said Minerva, frowning.

"Being a <u>real</u> grandmother has never been easy," said Babushka Ekaterina, her sorrowful eyes ringed by a sunburst of wrinkles. "But we do our best to pass on the wisdom of our Past."

"I don't think that's enough, anymore!"

"Neither do I," agreed Simone, whose wardrobe was always stylishly chic. "Times are changing, and so must we."

"But tradition is the backbone of what we do," objected Maria, her dark eyes flashing passionately. "Change could destroy that."

"It is possible to embrace new ideas without giving up the traditions that matter." Shizuka was wearing a beautiful kimono once worn by her grandmother, who had been a celebrated geisha.

"For some of us, that is harder to do," observed Babushka Ekaterina ruefully. She wore an old flowered kerchief, which was tied around her head peasant-style.

"What can we do?" asked Sophia, her hands suddenly still.

"That's something we all need to think about," replied Minerva. "But I think we should start with how we invest our money."

"Oh, but those statements and reports they send out are so complicated!" exclaimed Maria, rolling her 'rrr's emphatically.

"And too boring," yawned Sophia.

"I let my son handle such things for me," said Simone, adjusting her beret coquettishly.

"So did I! Until I realized what he was doing!" And Minerva told them what she had learned about the power of Money, and what she had done about it. All of them laughed and cheered her visit to The Club.

"My son belongs to one of those, too," said Simone, with her usual drollery. "Though it's not so stuffy and they do allow women – 'professional women', that is – at certain times."

"Maybe you, too, should pay your son a visit." Sophia arched her eyebrows and pretended to pout her lips.

"I think what you did was a good idea," said Maria, getting back to Minerva's plan. "But how did you ever figure out all that financial jargon?"

"It's not as hard as it looks," commented Shizuka. "But just as boring as it seems."

"I lost all my savings when the ruble was devalued." Babushka Ekaterina shook her head. "But I think Minerva has found a useful tactic for the rest of you. The others need to hear about this."

Babushka Ekaterina stood and waited. Almost immediately, everyone quieted down. Though it was a round room full of round tables – as befitted a group with no hierarchy – everyone recognized Ekaterina as their leader. For who knew more about being a grandmother than a Russian Babushka! "Minerva has something important she needs to discuss." Then she sat down and listened.

Minerva stood and looked around the room at her fellow grandmothers, and felt – as she always did – the strength of the deep bond which connected them. "As I'm sure all of you know, my granddaughter Valkira has recently started her training as a novice in our order." The grandmothers nodded; they all kept careful track of these things.

"She is a wonderful child, and has made remarkable progress," continued Minerva. "But she is encountering problems that none of us ever had to face. The outside world has become too dangerous for all our girls. What we are teaching them is not enough. We must do more. We must go back to the world and make it safer!"

A sustained note of concern in dozens of languages rippled around the room.

"We have Power! More than we realize! And we need to start using it more directly!"

"Hear! Hear!" murmured the grandmothers from Commonwealth Countries.

"Many of us own stock in the huge corporations that control too much of the world." Minerva's voice was strengthened by anger. "They are using their power to make the Earth unfit for our granddaughters!"

"What can we do?" shouted a woman with a British accent. "Surely we don't own enough stock for a corporate take-over!"

"That's true," agreed Minerva, "But if <u>all</u> of us owned just one share of stock, we could <u>all</u> attend the shareholders' meetings and tell them what we think!"

"I'll bet that would get their attention!" exclaimed a woman in a saffron-colored sari.

"Let's start with the Oil Companies!" suggested a woman in dark Muslim veils.

"Excellent idea!" Minerva was elated. "So let's do loaves-and-fishes. Anyone with more than one share of World Wide Petroleum, share with those who have none."

After much milling around and conferring, the grandmothers decided on where and when to congregate. Then they all gathered in a circle.

Minerva jumped on top of her table, raised her fist and shouted, "Grandmothers of the World, Unite!"

Everyone cheered. Some whistled and stamped their feet. Finally, Minerva led them in a rousing chorus of "The Grandmothers' Internationale."

Arise, ye grandmothers strong
Who want to right what is wrong.
Stand up now
And proclaim how
And sing our marching song!

For our granddaughters' sake,
It is time to awake!
Let's seize the hour
For Granny power
And make the world quake!

Long after the women had flown home, their passionate song echoed around the room.

Ω Ω Ω

The weather was rarely inclement in Minerva's backyard. Today the trees were waving with exceptional grace, and the flowers were expressing colors of extraordinary hue. Minerva leaned back in her dragon chaise lounge, a more mature version of Valkira's favorite chair. Katya and Koshka were both on her lap, purring in harmony. Olga was curled up at her feet, resting. Relaxing in the peaceful hum of her garden, Minerva reflected on the significance of her recent travels.

Going to stockholders meetings had been quite an adventure. Arriving unexpectedly at the first one, they had been met by middle managers who had absolutely no idea what to make of dozens of oddly dressed old women. The grandmothers sat down in front and listened politely. Then they started asking questions: "What are you doing about global warming? Why are you busting Unions? How much does your CEO make?" And so on.

At the meeting of the next corporation on their list, the middle managers tried to keep them out. Babushka Ekaterina scolded them sternly, and they sheepishly stepped aside. The grandmothers filed in and resumed their questioning: "Why don't you pay taxes? How many of your products are made in sweatshops? Why do you bank your profits in off-shore accounts?" And so on. And on.

But the next corporation was ready for them. Or so it thought. "We're sorry, but only major shareholders are allowed at this meeting," said a preppy-looking young man trying to sound authoritative. Lined up behind him were several burly young men, who definitely did not look like Ivy League graduates.

The grandmothers decided to hold a Protest, and sat down outside the entrance of the corporate headquarters. Eventually they were allowed in – but only after the meeting was over. The grandmothers returned – and came early – for the next one. This time, there were more guards – and more grandmothers. Once again, they were barred from the meeting; once again, they sat down to protest. But this time, they came prepared to stay. And – when they refused to move – the police were summoned to disperse them.

Some of the African-American grandmothers started singing "We Shall Overcome." As the others joined in, the police were ordered to make arrests. The women were furious! Babushka Ekaterina let loose a searing volley of eloquent Russian swearing. Sophia's vigorously gesticulating hands displayed a huge repertoire of obscene gestures. Shizuka even flipped a very subtle bird. The police eventually retreated, confused and shame-faced.

Remembering, Minerva smiled and decided that being Old had its advantages. *We can get away with a lot more now than when we were younger!*

Capitalizing on what had been a most unusual media event, the grandmothers held a press conference. They explained their purpose and announced a list of corporations they planned to visit. The Media, of course, eagerly followed. The grandmothers were terrific copy, and provided marvelous sound bites for the evening news. Their eccentric costumes and flying conveyances photographed extremely well.

Minerva herself had never liked having her picture taken. Olga, however, turned out to be a shameless publicity hound, and posed eagerly at every opportunity. Sophia and her mangy old camel also showed up in several photos. Olga grumbled that the ugly beast was cashing in on Sophia's cleavage. Which even Minerva admitted was rather unseemly for a woman her age.

Whether any of this would cause lasting change in corporate policy was debatable. But at least now everyone was thinking about it. And, Minerva noted with satisfaction, share prices of blue-chip stocks had declined markedly. Meanwhile, as more women followed Minerva's example and invested in Socially Responsible companies, their stock was rising. And the Congressional Women's Caucus had introduced a bill allowing tax credits to businesses which gave discounts to schools. Minerva was also urging a law that would make shareholders accountable for the malfeasance of corporations whose stocks they held.

Minerva was pleased with this progress, and gratified that more and more grandmothers – from all over the world – were joining The Movement.

If we work together and stand firm – We DO have Power!

More than anyone thinks!

Chapter 9

Fleur de Lily's

MINERVA WAS about to take off for another stockholders meeting and/or Protest – these days, one was never sure which – when she heard pounding on the gate to her garden.

"Grandmère!" shouted Valkira anxiously, "Grandmère, let us in! Please!"

Striding quickly to the gate, Minerva unlatched it.

Valkira burst into the garden, bristling with indignation, followed by Theodore and Ophelia. He, too, was angry, and she was almost in tears.

Minerva herded the distraught children onto the patio, and sat them down in their chairs. "Now, what is this all about?" she asked, in her most soothing calm-down voice.

"Ophelia's Mom has been fired from The Store!" exploded Valkira.

"Because she joined The Union!" added Theodore irately.

"And now we'll have to move again!" Ophelia started to cry.

"Can't she look for another job?" asked Minerva.

"Where?!" Valkira shook her head angrily. "The Store has undersold everyone else and driven all the other stores out of business!"

"Did anyone else get fired?" Minerva felt her temper rising.

"Just members of The Union!" replied Theodore.

"But that's illegal!" Minerva disappeared into her study and quickly returned, flipping thru pages of a thick portfolio. "Ah, yes – here it is. My share of stock in The Store. The Grandmothers will stage a Protest at the next stockholders meeting."

"But that will take too long!" Valkira shook her head. "Their landlord is threatening to evict them now!"

"Hmm, I see your point." Minerva sat down and thought about it.

"This is the first place we've lived long enough for me to make friends," sniffed Ophelia. "If only there were more places for Mom to work."

"Maybe some of those empty stores downtown will re-open." Theodore patted Ophelia's shoulder sympathetically.

"Selling what?!" Valkira shook her head again. "The Store can sell everything cheaper because it's all made SomeWhereElse!"

"That's it!" Minerva stood up suddenly. "Ophelia's Mom can make something RightHere that The Store doesn't sell – and re-open one of those empty shops."

"But The Store sells everything!" protested Valkira.

"It doesn't sell costumes! Not real Costumes!" argued Theodore. "Remember how Ophelia's Mom helped students make their Costumes for The Celebration?!"

"And Mom loved doing it!" Ophelia looked hopeful. "I've never seen her so happy!"

"And I'll bet a lot of people in town would rather wear her Costumes than those uniforms The Store calls fashion!" Valkira, too, was excited.

"But it takes money to start a business," cautioned Minerva. "And banks only lend money to people who already have some."

"Which Mom doesn't," sighed Ophelia.

"Maybe she could borrow money from someone besides a bank," suggested Theodore tentatively. "Someone who has lots more than she needs."

"Do you have someone in mind?" Minerva gave him a questioning look.

"Well, maybe," he replied hesitantly. "My parents are always talking about how much money my grandmother has, and complaining that she never spends any of it on them."

"Or on anyone else," added Valkira. "She's awfully stingy."

"Yes, I know," admitted Theodore. "But I think maybe she's just lonely – I'm the only one who ever visits her."

"Maybe if she weren't so crabby . . . ." muttered Valkira under her breath.

"Yes, I know," Theodore again admitted. "But she's really smart – and has nothing to do – and is bored."

"Maybe if she got involved in some interesting projects, she wouldn't be so bored." Minerva's eyes lit up. "And if it were a worthy cause, she might not be so crabby!"

"It wouldn't be easy persuading Gran to part with even a little of her money," said Theodore reluctantly. "All she talks about is saving money. For what, I don't know."

"Nonsense! I'll just invite her over and explain things to her!"

"Well – uh – I don't think that's such a good idea." Theodore shifted uncomfortably in his owl chair. "I think this place would freak her out."

"Then I'll go to her house."

"Well – uh – I don't think that would work either." Theodore hesitated. "She's pretty conservative and – well . . . ."

"She would never allow a 'dangerous radical' in her door." Valkira completed his thought, frowning.

"Then we'll accidentally meet some place neutral." Minerva sighed impatiently. "You pick the place and let me know when."

"OK, I think I can probably set something up. But – uh –" Theodore was treading very lightly now "– could you maybe – uh – dress – um – just a little more . . . ."

"Normal?" grinned Valkira wickedly.

"Hummph!" snorted Minerva.

"And bring Ophelia with you," he added. "But not Valkira!"

"Oh?" Minerva raised her eyebrows.

"I brought Valkira along last time I visited Gran . . . ."

"And . . . .?"

"They 'discussed' politics . . . ."

"I see." Minerva smiled and gave Valkira a proud hug.

Ω Ω Ω

After searching her closet for the third time, Minerva sighed. There was absolutely nothing there that Theodore's grandmother would NOT find objectionable.

Finally, she pulled out her most boring dress: a completely plain, very dark brown knit with straight-up-and-down lines that vaguely suggested an old Chanel design; its narrow skirt hung loosely but did not flow. Regarding herself in the mirror, she transformed her pendant and earrings into a single strand of pearls and small pearl studs. Twisting her long hair into a very careful chignon, she crowned it with her least flamboyant hat.

No, still too much. Minerva touched the brim, shortening it. *No, not enough.* She touched it again, lengthening the brim slightly on one side. *Better. Restrained but not ridiculous.* Since it was not a cold day, she reluctantly left her cape hanging on the coat rack in the hall.

Minerva met Ophelia at Moondeers, the popular new coffeehouse in town. It looked a bit too fast-foodish to feel like a real coffeehouse, but the coffee itself – though overpriced – wasn't bad.

Theodore and his grandmother arrived exactly on time. As they ordered their coffee, Minerva studied the other woman. She was almost tall and not quite fat, her widening waist probably restrained by uncomfortable undergarments Minerva herself had long since discarded. Her posture was erect and her carriage that of a Lady, with just enough gracious disdain to stop short of apparent snobbishness. The tailored black wool suit, the medium-heeled black pumps, the stylish hat with artfully arranged pheasant feathers atop carefully coiffed grey hair, the diamond jewelry of just the correct size on ears and fingers and around her neck, the expensive leather purse clutched protectively under one arm – all proclaimed OLD MONEY and GOOD TASTE. But the mink fur piece draped around her shoulders – made of four attached pelts, complete with eyes and nose, tail and paws – dated her fashionable ladyhood as several decades old.

Theodore – who of course had immediately spotted his friends in the corner – navigated his grandmother through the coffee line, and toward the table where Minerva and Ophelia were waiting.

"Oh, look who's here!" he exclaimed, with not very well feigned surprise. "Let's join them!"

Irritated, but smiling politely, grandmother followed grandson over to the table where two empty chairs just happened to be waiting.

"This is my grandmother, Morgana," said Theodore affectionately. "And this is Minerva, Valkira's grandmother."

Minerva stood up and extended her hand.

"Yes, I have already met her," said Morgana, clutching her purse with white gloved hands. "And I have seen you on TV, marching around with all those old women."

Minerva withdrew her proffered hand, deciding to interpret the rebuff as a throwback to when ladies never shook hands, rather than take offense. "You must be very proud of Theodore," she smiled instead. "He's such a fine boy."

"Everyone says I get my brains from Gran," interjected Theodore diplomatically.

"Then you must be very intelligent," said Minerva, following his lead, "because Theodore is a very smart boy!"

Morgana flushed at the unaccustomed compliment, fumbled with her purse, then sat down – just so – ankles crossed and skirt smoothed over her knees.

"This place is not quite what I expected," she said chattily, recovering her aplomb. "When I was in college, we visited a real coffeehouse in The Village – full of bearded sweaty beatniks spouting dreadful poetry."

Before Minerva could comment, Theodore once again demonstrated his skill as a diplomat.

"And this is Ophelia," he said hastily. "She's one of my best friends."

"Oh yes, the girl with the beautiful voice!" Morgana's glacial demeanor melted visibly in the warmth of Ophelia's smile. "I hope we shall hear you sing again soon!"

"Unfortunately, Ophelia's family may have to move." Minerva made use of the opening. "For financial reasons."

"Oh dear, was your father transferred?' asked Morgana sympathetically. "I know how hard that is. My late husband uprooted us every time he got a promotion."

"No, it's not Dad," replied Ophelia quietly, her smile fading. "It's my Mom – she got fired from The Store."

"Oh well – that is not such a nice place to work anyway. Now she can stay home and bake brownies for you after school."

"That's not an option!" cut in Minerva, trying to keep the edge off her voice. "If she doesn't work, there's no money for brownies – or anything else."

"Oh, but I thought . . . ." Morgana stopped, the confusion on her face turning first into embarrassment, then to self-righteous disapproval.

Both women opened their mouths, each about to launch the first volley of what most certainly would have been a confrontation of significant proportions.

But Theodore once again intervened strategically. "The problem, Gran, is that since The Store has a monopoly on what's sold here in town, there are no other jobs available. But Ophelia's Mom would like to open her own business."

"Oh, what a fine idea!" Back on familiar entrepreneurial ground, Morgana turned, with relief, to Ophelia. "What kind of business?"

And Ophelia proceeded to explain: about the Costumes for the Celebration, how much her mother had enjoyed making them, how important it was to have clothes that say who you really are, how it affects the way other people see you and how you feel about yourself. As she talked, Ophelia's eyes glowed with irresistible enthusiasm. "The Store only sells uniforms made SomeWhereElse. I think lots of people RightHere would buy Mom's Costumes!"

"So do I, my dear!" exclaimed Morgana, reflecting Ophelia's excitement. "So do I!"

"All she needs is a small loan to get started," said Theodore. "But the banks won't give her one because she has no collateral."

Looking from Ophelia's eager face to the pleading look in her grandson's eyes, Morgana blanched. "Surely you are not suggesting . . . ." she gasped, after a long horrified pause.

"Please, Gran, you'd be doing something really good for some really good people."

"But I have to save my money! I cannot just spend it . . . . Not just to help people!"

"But why not? You have way more than you'll ever need."

"But it is not good business . . . ."

"Yes, it is!" interrupted Minerva, deciding it was time to play her trump card. "Theodore tells me that J.P. Morgan, the great banker and financier, was your great-grandfather."

"Yes, that is true," replied Morgana proudly. "I was named for him."

"Surely he did not make so much money by having it sit idly in his banks?!"

"Well, no . . . ."

"And my son the banker tells me that on more than one occasion, J.P. used his money to help the nation avert a Depression."

"Well, yes . . . ."

"Maybe it's time for the House of Morgan to rise again – and save the town!"

"Well, maybe . . . ."

There was a spark in Morgana's eyes her grandson had never seen there before.

"I have an idea, Gran," he said excitedly. "Let Ophelia's Mom make you a Costume. Then you can see what a great idea this is!"

Morgana nodded. The expression on her face made clear how much she hoped her skepticism could be overcome.

Ω Ω Ω

As Ophelia and Lily walked into the lobby of Morgana's ultra-posh condo building, both of them were nervous.

Lily was a slight, fragile-featured woman, who would have been pretty without the mantle of fear lurking overhead. She was wearing a Costume she had just made for herself. The cream-colored dress of light cotton gauze flowed softly around her slim body, the sleeves and skirt flared at the bottom and edged with petal-like points the color of harvested corn. On her short hair was a small matching cap of petals which accentuated the wisps framing her gentle face. Around her neck was a small woven cord of green macramé, on which hung a ceramic fleur de lis. Small gold lilies also dangled from her ears.

"You look beautiful, Mom!" said Ophelia, as she rang the buzzer.

"I hope she thinks so!" replied Lily in an unsteady voice.

Theodore met them at the door, smiling encouragingly, and ushered them into the large, expensively decorated living room where Morgana was holding court. Authentic antique bric-a-brac adorned heavy Victorian furniture resting on thick oriental carpets; there was just enough space in between so that the room did not quite look cluttered. Morgana herself was sitting in a large throne-like chair behind a coffee table, on which rested a massively ornate silver service. Two uncomfortable-looking vintage settees flanked the table. She was wearing a long black satin hostess gown reminiscent of 1940s movies; her perfectly combed grey page-boy was adorned with a matching headband to which a tasteful diamond brooch was affixed.

Morgana nodded graciously to her visitors, and indicated one of the settees with a majestic gesture. Despite her nervousness, Lily walked gracefully across the huge room and perched on the edge of the velvet upholstery. Ophelia sat down close beside her.

Morgana poured tea into delicate bone china cups, added sugar with sterling spoons monogrammed with a large M, and balanced the saucers on a elegantly extended hand. The large diamonds on her fingers flashed opulently.

Lily accepted the cup with hands bare of adornment – and which miraculously did not tremble. Feeling Morgana's scrutinizing gaze, Lily took several deep breaths and then met the older woman's eyes. In them she read patronizing appreciation of her Costume, and behind that, a huge wall of condescension.

After a polite exchange of limping small talk, the thin china cups were returned to the thick silver tray. Morgana looked at Theodore and, with an imperious wave, pointed toward a door on one side of the room.

Theodore, urged on by Lily's obvious discomfort and Ophelia's imploring eyes, hurried into the next room and quickly returned with a large box. Carefully he deposited it at his grandmother's feet.

"Theodore said that you would want to see some personal objects especially important to me," Morgana said, as she turned to Lily.

Lily nodded, and focused on the box.

"Many of these things belonged to my famous great-grandfather, J.P. Morgan," said Morgana proudly. "He was a very wealthy banker, you know."

"So I've heard," said Lily, pushing the condescension aside.

One by one, Morgana exhibited her inherited treasures: a silver rimmed pince-nez, a platinum pocket watch, an ebony walking stick with a small silver globe on top, a coin collection of mint silver Morgan dollars and Mercury dimes, and a black silk top-hat worn by the great J.P. himself. Morgana reverently placed the hat on her head – then impulsively tilted it slightly.

Blushing, she hastily removed the hat and placed it on the coffee table – where it seemed quite at ease beside the silver service.

Reaching again into the box, Morgana carefully unfolded a black pin-striped formal cutaway coat. "My father wore this when he argued cases before the Supreme Court." She looked longingly at the old garment, palpably invested with memories of long ago.

Finally she refolded the coat, and lifted one more item from the bottom of the box. "And this is where he carried his briefs for those court appearances." Resting the black leather attaché case on her knees, Morgana stroked it lovingly – and regretfully.

"Why are these things so important to you?" asked Lily gently, her antennae honed in on them, picking up powerful vibes.

"Because," said Morgana finally, "they remind me of who I was supposed to be."

"I understand," said Lily, seeing the sadness in her eyes.

And Morgana, seeing the compassion in Lily's eyes, knew that she did.

They were all silent while Morgana packed away her memories.

"And now," said Lily, after the box was closed, "I need to see your clothes closet."

Ophelia and Theodore waited in the living room while Morgana led Lily through an enormous bedroom into the largest closet Lily had ever seen. *This is almost as big as our whole apartment!* She stared at all the racks and shelves, and was amazed that all the clothes were hung and stacked in perfect order. *Has she nothing better to do?!*

After a few hours of perusing Morgana's huge expensive wardrobe, Lily picked out several items: a pair of loose-fitting black gabardine slacks styled à la Katharine Hepburn, a grey boiled wool vest, a collar of silver fox fur, a pair of white kid gloves, a pair of low-heeled patent leather pumps. And finally, from a long rack of perfectly ironed identical garments, an immaculate long-sleeved white cotton blouse.

A week later, Morgana's Costume was ready.

Both women were excited as she tried it on.

"You know," said Morgana, putting on the Katharine Hepburn slacks Lily had enlarged at the waist, "these were considered very daring, back then." After fastening the sleeves of the white blouse with cufflinks made from silver Mercury dimes, she put on the grey vest, and slipped her feet into the low-heeled black patent shoes.

Lily then held up her masterpiece: an updated version of the Supreme Court cutaway coat. Tailored and black and pin-striped, it looked impressively official yet still flowed with a hint of elegant ladyhood. And it fit perfectly. Morgana was thrilled.

"And now for the accessories!" Lily, too, was pleased. A brooch made from a Morgan silver dollar fastened the blouse collar; the platinum watch was tucked into the pocket of the vest and the pince-nez placed inside the breast pocket of the coat. After Morgana pulled on the white kid gloves, Lily gave her the walking stick with the silver globe and handed her the black leather attaché case.

"And now the finishing touch!" Lily presented a modified version of J.P.'s top hat. The crown was shorter, the brim wider, and wrapped around the black felt was a silver fur band. Ceremoniously she placed it on Morgana's head.

Regarding herself in the long mirror, Morgana felt transformed. Her body stood taller, shoulders back, head up, stance widened, feet angled out. It was her – but so much more.

"How do you feel?" asked Lily.

"POWERFUL!" exclaimed Morgana. "Like who I was meant to be!"

Finally, she turned and looked levelly at Lily. "Thank you."

Instead of condescension, Lily saw only respect.

Morgana held out her hand. "Do we have a deal?"

Lily smiled and slowly shook Morgana's hand. "Partners?"

"Partners!"

Ω Ω Ω

"This is the Place!" exclaimed Lily.

"It'll be just perfect!" Ophelia echoed her excitement.

They had been there all morning, planning how everything would look. And now they were giving Minerva and Valkira, Theodore and Morgana the tour.

Lily had found an empty shop in the middle of the street that had once been the downtown's prime retail location. All the stores had been vacant for too long; they looked lonely and worn out.

Standing inside the front door, the grandmothers and grandchildren looked around. The first floor was spacious, divided in the middle by a large staircase, which led up to a wide balcony extending around three sides of the interior. Everything was littered with debris.

"Oh dear," sighed Morgana. "What a mess!"

"Yes, that's true," said Minerva, trying hard not to sound dismayed. "But look at all that beautiful wood underneath. I'll bet it's solid oak." Walking over to the staircase, she pushed aside a collapsed ceiling tile and revealed a carved bannister with brown paint starting to flake away. "See? When we've stripped away all that ugly paint, it'll be beautiful!"

After uncovering oak floors that were also solid, Minerva's natural optimism reasserted itself. Morgana, dressed in her usual ladyhood outfit, remained skeptical. Though she tried on her Costume every day in front of her bedroom mirror, she had not yet mustered the courage to wear it in public. Minerva, meanwhile, was garbed in her usual flowing dress and cape and big hat. Morgana averted her eyes, and endeavored unsuccessfully to contain her disapproval.

The children, meanwhile, had caught their friend's enthusiasm and listened avidly as Lily described where everything would be.

"Over here, on the right, as you walk into the store, is where we'll keep all the old clothes and things we'll recycle into Costumes. Racks along the walls, tables and shelves in the middle. Up there," she pointed to the balcony above, "will be my workshop – cutting table, sewing machine, shelves with supplies and such. And, of course, fitting rooms. And – oh yes – in that cozy corner will be a comfortable consultation space where people can tell me who they are and what kind of Costume they want."

"What about the rest of the place?" Morgana's fretful voice interrupted.

I'll bet she's worrying about how much it's going to cost! Valkira was annoyed.

"Mom and I decided that we might just as well live here, too," replied Ophelia enthusiastically. "Upstairs in the back are two rooms we can turn into bedrooms. And there's a plumbing hook-up for a bathroom in between."

"And downstairs?" gasped Morgana, mentally adding prices in her head.

"Over on the left side will be a living room/dining area that can double as a place to entertain customers. In back we'll put a kitchen next to the bathroom already there."

"And what about up there?" Morgana pointed to the balcony above.

"That will be Ophelia's space," replied Lily. "She's going to recycle things that make music. And hopefully it will also become a place where she and her friends will make their own music, too!"

By this time, everyone except Morgana was seeing the store as it would become.

"Have you thought about how much money this is going to cost?" she asked, choking with apprehensive frugality.

"Not as much as you think," replied Lily, putting a soothing hand on the tense arm with which Morgana clutched her purse. "Trust me."

Morgana looked at the glowing faces around her – and was surprised how much she wanted to see what they saw. Taking a deep breath, she loosened her grip on the purse and looked up the stairway.

Suddenly the debris was gone. The golden oak of the gracefully carved bannisters glowed, and on the mellow wooden steps stood several whimsical mannequins dressed in wonderfully creative Costumes.

An enormous smile spread over Morgana's face as she took a huge leap of faith. "Well," she grinned, feeling genuinely happy for the first time in years, "I guess it's only money."

Ω Ω Ω

It did, of course, take several weeks for the shop to actually become the vision in the eyes of the beholders.

First Mr. Hammerstein, Industrial Ed teacher at Jane Addams Junior High, brought his advanced class to help fix the plumbing and heating and electrical wiring. Necessary materials for repair were charged to his Education Supplies budget in return for giving his students a chance to practice what he was teaching.

Lily and Minerva went to work stripping innumerable layers of paint from the solid oak floors and woodwork. They then repainted all the walls in several bright colors. The children, meanwhile, patrolled the streets before trash pick-up and after garage sales, hunting for cast-off furniture and appliances. They also cruised affluent neighborhoods, offering to clean out and haul away junk from the basements. Mr. Marcheson delivered what they found in the band's equipment van, which the School Board had surprised him with after Valkira's big half-time show.

Theodore invited his gang of ex-bullies to help fix up the old furniture and repair the appliances. Ashley brought friends from her dance class to make decorative curtains and cushions from old sheets and bedspreads.

Morgana initiated a clothing drive by encouraging the other wealthy widows in her condo building to clean out their closets. And she even donated an antique round oak table with matching chairs and buffet. "It looks so much better with all this wonderful woodwork than it did in my storage unit!" she exclaimed, enjoying the unaccustomed thrill of generosity.

"I'll bet that's the first time she's ever given anything away!" grinned Valkira. But not so Morgana could hear.

As the shop began to resemble the vision, Morgana's visits became more frequent. Always, of course, to 'supervise' her investment. Ladies, after all, never got their hands dirty. Occasionally she conversed with Minerva, who was always there, getting her hands dirty in all kinds of unladylike ways.

"Why do you do it?" Morgana asked, watching Minerva paint an old dresser for Ophelia's bedroom.

"Do what?" Minerva itched her nose and left a smudge of paint on it.

"Oh, you know, march around and bother all those corporations."

"We're trying to convince them to do business responsibly and not be so greedy." Minerva finished applying the second coat of blue paint and left it to dry.

"But they have to make a profit so that money can trickle down to everyone else," protested Morgana.

"Except that it usually doesn't." Minerva moved to the matching blue headboard – now dry – and started painting a large yellow circle in the middle. "There are better ways to feed the birds than by giving the horses more oats."

"Like what?" Morgana grimaced at the earthy metaphor.

"Well, like what we're doing here." Minerva paused, paintbrush in mid-air, and thought about it. "OK, you're lending Lily money so she can start her own business, right?"

Morgana nodded.

"Hopefully she'll earn enough from it to live on. But she'll need to spend that money on things she can't make herself."

"So she will go to The Store because the prices are lowest there."

"Only because workers SomeWhereElse aren't paid enough to live decently." Minerva emphasized her point, paintbrush still in hand. A glob of yellow paint narrowly missed the dead minks around Morgana's shoulders. "BUT if she bought from other local businesses, those people could earn enough to live on and also spend locally, round and round, until there were more jobs for everyone."

"But those local businesses do not exist anymore, so she will still have to go to The Store," objected Morgana, moving out of the paint's line of fire. "And I will still get my stock dividend."

"OR," Minerva pointed the paintbrush at the black leather attaché case Morgana had recently started using as a purse, "you could take the interest Lily pays you, and lend it to other people to start more local businesses."

"Hmmm."

"Wouldn't that be more fun for everyone?" Minerva finished painting the headboard. "You might even make more money than from The Store's stock dividends."

Ω Ω Ω

During the day, Lily's shop was full of people enthusiastically helping to refurbish it. Just before dark, they all went home. Lily and Ophelia, who had already moved in, were left alone. Minerva was always the last to leave, and noticed that though Lily tried to hide it, she always looked afraid when she said goodbye.

"Mom got really scared last night," confided Ophelia one morning. "The back door came unlatched and was banging in the wind. We thought it was . . . . Well, we were both scared."

"This place could use a good watchdog," said Minerva, who had also been concerned about something like that happening.

"A dog? A dog!!" Ophelia's face lit up. "Oh, I've always wanted a dog!"

Shortly before Opening Day, Ophelia went to the Animal Shelter. In a cage way in the back was a large, exceptionally homely mongrel whose fur was a kaleidoscope of colors and textures.

Ophelia was, of course, immediately drawn to him. He looked appealingly at her out of big, sad eyes.

"What kind of dog is that?" she asked, noticing that one ear was floppy, while the other pointed and perked.

"He's a combination of every breed I've ever seen," replied the keeper. "And seems to have all their worst traits. Even when I feed him, he's surly."

The man quickly shoved some food into the cage. The dog snarled viciously.

"We'll probably have to put him to sleep." The keeper shook his head. "Nobody wants such an ugly, nasty animal!"

"Well, I do!" said Ophelia

"Listen, Miss, he might hurt you!"

"No, he won't! He has all the <u>best</u> traits of all those breeds, too!" Ophelia held out her hand.

The dog approached quietly, tail wagging, eyes beseeching, and knelt docilely at her feet.

"What is your name?" she asked politely.

He pointed his muzzle in the air and howled melodiously.

Ophelia beamed and opened the cage. "I'm happy to meet you, Wolf."

The dog followed her obediently home.

It soon became apparent that although Wolf was undeniably the most unattractive dog ever created, he was very intelligent and talented. He was strong, a hard worker, eager to be helpful, and immediately made himself useful by fetching tools, pushing heavy things into place, snipping whatever needed cutting with his powerful jaws, pulling anything that needed to be carried in whatever conveyance was at hand. He even took out the garbage every night – without being reminded. Although no one could ever call him cute, Wolf quickly perceived that the patient earnestness with which he cocked his mismatched ears never failed to charm. And he was absolutely devoted to Ophelia and Lily. Every night he slept at the door, guarding the entrance zealously.

Wolf's loyalty soon endeared him to everyone. Except Morgana. Who proclaimed him a "Filthy Beast!" the moment she laid eyes on him.

Wolf growled. But did not move.

"How could you bring such an ugly animal into this beautiful place!?!" Morgana was utterly appalled.

And then, one night, she understood.

The shop was finally ready for its Grand Opening. Morgana stopped by the night before to wish Lily and Ophelia good luck. Wolf was busy taking out the garbage. Everyone else had gone home.

As she opened the front door, Morgana saw a strange man starting unsteadily up the stairway toward Lily and Ophelia, cowering at the top.

"Who are you?!" demanded Morgana, quickly accosting him. "What are you doing here?!"

The man turned and looked blearily at her. "Min' yer own bus'ness, Ol' Woman!" he shouted, swaying. His words slurred and his breath reeked of alcohol.

"Get out of here!" Morgana shouted.

The man shoved her, and she fell against the bannister. Then he lurched up the steps toward Lily and Ophelia, who both screamed.

Suddenly, from the back door under the stairs, a huge snarling Wolf, teeth bared and eyes wild, fur bristling every which way, hurtled through the air and knocked over the intruder. Standing on his chest, powerful jaws around the man's throat, Wolf looked up at Ophelia.

Inspired by his ferocious strength, Ophelia walked slowly down the stairs. With each step, she felt anger chasing away her fear. "Swear!" she said, standing over the terrified man, "Swear! That you will NEVER bother us again!"

"I jus' wan' wha's mine!" he grunted.

Wolf growled and tightened his grip.

Stunned by the wonder of his protective loyalty, Lily felt years of terror melting away. "Nothing here belongs to you anymore!" she exclaimed, joining Ophelia at the bottom of the staircase. "Now get out!"

At Ophelia's signal, Wolf released his grip.

"And stay out!" shouted Lily after him, as he staggered away on unsteady legs.

"Are you OK?" Lily helped Morgana to her feet.

"I am fine. Was that . . . ?"

"Yes." There were tears in Lily's eyes. But, for the first time, no fear.

Morgana looked at Lily with new understanding. And at Wolf with new eyes.

Tentatively she turned to the dog, nervously extended her hand, and awkwardly patted his head.

Wolf wagged his tail and cocked his ears endearingly.

"I was wrong, Wolf." Morgana smiled. "You are a magnificent dog!"

Ω Ω Ω

On Opening Day, FLEUR de LILY's exceeded everyone's hopes and dreams.

The sign over the front door had been painted by Ms. Rembrandt's art class in gold script bordered by multi-colored lilies. In one display window hung stars with pictures of the Celebration cast in their Costumes. In the other window was Ophelia's lyre, couched in veils and flowers, and surrounded by drawings of several exotic musical instruments.

Inside, the ceiling and walls were painted all the colors of the rainbow. The overhanging pipes and fixtures had also been painted as a bright counterpoint to the multi-colored background. The varnished oak floors glowed with a soft golden sheen.

The right half of the main floor was ringed by racks hung with old clothing of numerous fabrics and styles and sizes. In the middle were variously-shaped wooden crates painted in earth tones, on which were displayed a wide assortment of shoes, hats, belts, gloves, canes, and umbrellas. Old trunks overflowed with feathers and plumes, garlands and sashes. Rebuilt shelves were lined with reused gift boxes filled with discarded holiday ornaments.

In the balcony above was Lily's workshop. In the center was a large cutting table, fashioned from two old doors, carefully sanded, set upon sawhorses painted green and sprinkled with pale gold glitter. Next to it, under the skylight, was the only object in the entire building that was not recycled: a brand-new, state-of-the-art sewing machine presented to Lily by Morgana.

Along one wall were floor-to-ceiling shelves filled with sequins and beads and glitter, yarn and ribbon and cord, old buttons and gilt chains and faux gems, and innumerable spools of thread of every conceivable hue. On the opposite wall was a row of fitting rooms, each closeted by a bright green curtain appliquéd with a large gold fleur de lis. In between was a cozily exotic sitting area. On an old area rug of emerald, sapphire and ruby shag, stood three over-stuffed chairs re-upholstered in matching colors. They were clustered around a small elliptical coffee table, strategically positioned to mask a large bald spot in the carpet. The table top was inlaid with shards of green, blue and red bottles; a canopy of dyed gold mosquito netting was suspended from spiral-shaped mobiles of discarded copper wire.

The balcony on the other side had a purposely unfinished look. Next to an old upright piano and a box of music stands, leaned several folding chairs. On the adjacent wall were board-and-brick shelves waiting for more sheet-music and CD's; in the center shelf was a repaired CD player with large speakers. On the floor was a plain round area rug, upon which was a circle of multi-colored sitting cushions matching the walls.

"Music is always a work-in-progress," explained Ophelia to Morgana, who was regarding the space thru J.P.'s pince-nez. Hanging around her neck on a long silver chain, it was a handy prop for delaying judgment on things newly encountered and not yet understood.

Back downstairs, on the left side of the stairs, was a simply furnished, very comfortable seating area which cordially invited conversation. In the corner where the edges met, two re-upholstered couches right angled around a square lamp table. Lengthwise, they enclosed a pie-shaped coffee table; several cushions lined up along its rounded edge on the rug extending beyond. The carpet had also been rounded off.

Next to the conversation space, Morgana's donated dining table harmonized happily with the mellow oak floor; the buffet against the wall and the chairs flanking the table also looked content to be back on their own turf. The kitchen in the back was shielded by a large folding screen on which Ms. Rembrandt's students had painted especially fanciful designs that artfully integrated all the colors in the living area.

Morgana had arrived very early that morning, changed immediately into her Costume, and spent several hours walking about getting used to it. She soon discovered ways of manipulating the accessories to good effect. Taking out the pocket watch, gazing pointedly at it, then snapping it shut was a tactful way of indicating impatience. Peering at the unknown through the pince-nez was a safe way of making ignorance appear to be wisdom. And grasping the walking stick firmly under one arm was a tacit way of claiming dominance.

Minerva arrived much later, not long before the doors were to open. She, too, had dressed up for the occasion. Her usual long gown and cape were of bright royal blue velvet, and flowed even more than usual. The sapphires in her pendant and earrings were significantly larger. And her hat was huge, with an extra wide brim and abundant plumes.

As she swept into the room, she greeted Morgana – who immediately reached for her pince-nez. After a long look, she firmly grasped her ebony walking stick; on its silver globe was etched a dollar sign. Pointing it at Minerva, she struck a pose worthy of J.P. Morgan.

Minerva took note, and smiled rather wickedly. In her hand suddenly appeared an even more elegant walking stick, much like those seen in portraits of 17th-century European nobility. It was noticeably taller than Morgana's. Minerva, too, struck an aristocratic pose, and inclined her staff in such a way that Morgana could not miss the abstract peace sign gracefully encircling its gold globe.

Overhead in the balcony, Valkira and Theodore burst into laughter. Both grandmothers looked up and glared.

At that moment, Lily fortunately appeared. She was wearing a formal version of the Costume in which she had initially visited Morgana. The skirt was full-length, the colors deeper and more vivid, and a wreath of lilies crowned her head. Gracefully she descended to the landing midway down the stairway. Ophelia, dressed in her own Costume, joined her there. Flanking them at the bottom stood Minerva, on the left, and Morgana, on the right.

The stairway itself was a magnificent cascade of solid oak, its venerable beauty glowing like a beloved old song. Leaning against the curving bannisters and balcony railings above were several mannequin-like sculptures; each was ingeniously crafted from odds and ends of brooms and pipes and lampshades and such, and all were dressed in festive ensembles of garments donated from the closets of Morgana's wealthy friends.

When it was time, Wolf opened the doors and started herding the people waiting outside toward the entrance. Ophelia began to sing. Valkira *Ohm . . . Ohmm . . . Ohmmm'*d into her purple cape and horns. Theodore *Hoo . . . Hooo . . . Hoooo*ted into his owl feathers. As they leaped off the balcony and swooped over the staircase, Minerva raised her staff. Warm light the color of amber poured forth, joining Ophelia's song and suffusing the room. FLEUR de LILY's was filled with pure happiness – and the comforting smell of baking bread.

Chapter 10

The Co-op

Once Fleur de Lily's was up and running, Morgana brought her best friends to see it.

Constance, Patience, Temperance, and Chastity were part of a club with whom Morgana had played canasta for years. The group met every Tuesday at the Senior Center in the basement of their condo building. Though at first glance the old ladies were of various sizes and shapes and dressed in different colors, they soon assumed the homogeneous guise of grey ladyhood in the eyes of anyone beholding them; almost immediately, it was impossible to tell them apart.

Morgana herself was dressed in the black ladyhood uniform in which she had first met Minerva and Ophelia at the coffeehouse. Her friends were similarly garbed in expensive, slightly outmoded ensembles, complete with the proper amount of costly jewelry. All wore tasteful little hats and clutched overly large leather purses with white-gloved hands.

The ladies smiled nervously as Morgana ushered them in. She, too, was apprehensive as she watched their reaction to her investment. As they looked around, horror and delight did visible combat on their faces. In the end, confused curiosity prevailed.

"Well," said Constance, as politely as she could, "this is certainly an interesting place."

"Yes," agreed Temperance, trying unsuccessfully to contain her shock, "and the colors are so bright."

"And those costumes are certainly daring." Chastity's voice mingled disapproval and wistfulness.

"Maybe," added Patience, both doubtfully and hopefully, "one gets used to it."

Morgana smiled to herself as Lily gracefully descended the stairway in the most conservative version of her signature Costume. After proudly showing the visitors around her establishment, she seated them in the conversation area. Ophelia served them green tea and sang. The ladies were charmed.

Meanwhile, one by one, Lily took them up to the consultation space in her workshop. Each of them ascended the stairs with careful propriety; all of them descended with varying degrees of tentative delight.

A week later, the ladies returned. This time, Morgana greeted them in her J.P. Costume. They all tried not to stare.

"Well," said Constance, "that certainly is an interesting outfit."

"Yes," agreed Temperance, mildly disappointed, "but the colors aren't very bright."

"But it certainly is daring," added Chastity hopefully.

"And not too hard to get used to," grinned Patience, in an almost unladylike fashion.

"Just wait!" exclaimed Minerva, and led them up to the main fitting room where Lily awaited. As each of the old ladies stepped behind the green curtain, shocked silence gave way to squeals of delight. Then, after an apprehensive pause, each emerged and unveiled her new persona.

Chastity was the first to step out. Her ample figure was clad in an A-line calf-length jumper, black with a wide red ruffle at the hem. Its slimming lines fitted becomingly over a red silk turtleneck and flowed gracefully over black leather boots with taps. Draped over her shoulders was a black lace cape lined in red. On her head was a black satin Zorro-style hat adorned with a large red rose. Around her neck was a red cord on which hung a pair of castanets. And sprinkled lavishly over the entire ensemble were handfuls of red sequins.

Chastity stood before the mirror on the wall, regarding herself as though at a stranger. Slowly she raised the castanets over her head, arched her back, and tapped her feet. "Olé!" she exclaimed, clicking the castanets and stomping her boots again.

Next to emerge was Temperance, who was the shortest of the four ladies. A bright pink leotard encased her proudly petite upper body; a knee-length multi-colored tutu disguised her astonishingly large hips. Matching pink tights covered her calves, and on her feet were wine-colored ballet slippers laced with gilded ribbons. Her light blond greying hair was fastened in a taupe chignon surrounded by a coronet of multi-colored rhinestones. The layers of her tutu were all of different hues and adorned with sparkling sequins.

Gazing at her reflection, Temperance grinned with huge satisfaction. Humming a Tchaikovsky waltz, she did a graceful pirouette.

Constance was next. A floor-length royal blue sheath dress made her tall, gaunt body appear stylishly chic. The gown was topped with a matching straw hat with tall crown and large sloping brim. Around her neck and wrists, on her fingers and dangling from her ears glittered rhinestones in happy profusion. Oversized sunglasses and a long cigarette holder completed her accessories.

Constance made a few runway turns, struck a model-like stance, then looked over her shoulder into the mirror. "Mo - o - on River . . . ." she crooned huskily. The flashlight at the end of the faux cigarette holder blinked in rhythm.

Finally it was the turn of Patience, who strode out in black stretch pants, silver leather boots, and a black turtleneck emblazoned with a silver-sequined eagle. On her head was a modified aviator's hood and above her eyes were matching goggles, both generously embellished with silver glitter. Over her broad shoulders was an ankle-length black leather vest on which marched several lines of silver studs.

Patience confronted the mirror, widening her stance and squaring her shoulders. "Born to be WI - I - I - ILD . . . ." she belted out with lots of <u>very</u> unladylike attitude.

For the rest of the afternoon, the women walked about Fleur de Lily's, gazing in mirrors, fine-tuning accessories, getting the feel of their Costumes. Chastity stomped and clicked a lot, Temperance pirouetted energetically in her tutu, Constance waved and pointed her cigarette holder imperiously, Patience practiced assertive stances that swirled her vest impressively. Finally they all sat down in the conversation area.

"Well," began Morgana, "How do you feel?"

"Not like me," replied Chastity.

"Not like the old me, anyway," said Temperance.

"More like a new me," added Constance.

"Who is more than the old me," concluded Patience.

"Then maybe you all need new names," suggested Lily, setting a bucket of champagne on the coffee table.

"Hear! Hear!" exclaimed Morgana, as her friends excitedly considered the matter.

Finally, after a great deal of good-natured discussion, each lady was ready to reveal her new name.

"Call me Carmen!" said Chastity, clicking and stomping.

"And I am now Belle!" exclaimed Temperance, flouncing her tutu purposefully.

"Audrey here, if you please!" announced Constance, striking a charmingly modish pose.

"And my name is Ventura!" concluded Patience, putting hands on hips.

As the group applauded, Lily poured champagne all around.

"A toast!" proclaimed Morgana, raising her glass. "To the ladies we were – and the women we <u>are</u>!"

All of them drained their glasses – and cheered like Women!

Ω Ω Ω

None of them – not even Morgana – dared wear their Costumes home. And certainly not to the Tuesday Canasta Club.

"I miss my Costume," sniffed Carmen née Chastity.

"So do I," sighed Belle née Temperance, "But I wouldn't feel comfortable wearing it here."

"Nor would I," agreed Audrey née Constance. "We need to go someplace else. Someplace new."

"And we need to do something new," concluded Ventura née Patience. "I'm tired of playing canasta!"

"Well, then," suggested Morgana, "why not go into business – like Lily did?"

The women née ladies discussed the matter all afternoon, and thought about it all week.

At the next week's meeting of the Canasta Club, they all showed up with business plans in hand – and in their Costumes. The other ladies stared. The five women walked out – never to return.

Ω Ω Ω

Carmen rented the store next to Lily's place; her plan was to sell repaired and redecorated old furniture. Next door was Belle, whose intention was to create original home décor from discarded fabric and interesting trash. On the other side of Fleur de Lily's was Audrey's recycled jewelry store. And next to her was Ventura's used bookstore.

Across the street, Morgana took over the old bank building. Since all of her friends had borrowed money from her to start their enterprises, she needed a place from which to monitor her investments. Carefully refurbishing all the elegant old fixtures, she created a space that set off her J.P. garb to perfection. And in the new office, the authoritative gestures implicit in the Costume's accessories were honed to the point where she almost felt like the great J.P. himself.

All of the erstwhile little old ladies threw themselves into their respective endeavors with energy and zest worthy of the new women they were becoming. But they soon discovered that some assistance from younger hands – and backs – was needed.

"They should ask their grandkids to help them," said Theodore, who had been helping Morgana clean up the old bank.

"But all of them live too far away," replied Ophelia, who had been trying to assist all of her new neighbors.

"Then we should find them some foster grandchildren," suggested Valkira. "A lot of kids at school don't have nearby grandmothers, either. Let's match them up!"

After careful consideration and mutual interviewing, those without grandmothers connected with those without grandchildren. Ashley and Belle hit it off immediately, as did Stacey and Audrey. C.Chaplin was soon helping Carmen move furniture around. And, when it was discovered that Ms. Anthony, too, was grandmotherless, Ventura adopted her. It was quickly decided that the recently unemployed teacher would offer history and geography seminars at the Used Bookstore.

Belle and Ashley soon created fanciful displays of cleverly appliquéd pillows and embroidered wall hangings and beaded lampshades. Carmen and C.Chaplin designed a line of brightly painted loft beds, fold-away tables, and other space-saving furniture. Audrey and Stacey designed highly original costume jewelry and painstakingly layered lacquer boxes in which to keep it. Ventura and Ms. Anthony brought to life books about far-away places and times with parties at which they dressed in foreign garb and served exotic food.

As enthusiasm mounted, the excitement spread. In the store next to Morgana's bank, Albert and his gang of ex-bullies rejuvenated broken appliances with energy-efficient motors, and set up a windmill that provided electricity for all the shops on the street. In the store on the other side of the bank, Eugene and members of the track team repaired and custom-decorated bicycles. They also designed attached conveyances for Senior Citizens who had lost their drivers' licenses. Elijah and the football team provided pedal power, and wore helmets that matched the whimsical shapes and colors of the improvised rickshaws.

Ophelia and Wolf made many visits to the Animal Shelter, where they liberated several dogs of various breeds. Wolf organized his canine corps carefully, assigning members the tasks for which they had been bred. Huskies pulled carts for hauling supplies, Border Collies directed traffic, Labradors retrieved lost items, German Shepherds policed the streets, a large St. Bernard provided First Aid. Food and lodging for the dogs were provided by all the merchants of The Co-op, as everyone was now calling it.

In organizing the Co-op Canine Corps, Wolf was ably assisted by Olga. The two dogs shared a similar work ethic, and soon became close friends. Wolf, of course, was multi-lingual and was thus able to communicate with Olga in her native tongue.

"His accent is rather strange," she confided to Minerva, "But his Russian is very charming."

Noting the fond look in Olga's eyes, Minerva smiled.

Olga also confided concern for the mental health of the members of The Co-op. "Wolf thinks that with business increasing, so is the stress level of the humans who work here."

"Hmmm," remarked Minerva, "Wolf is quite the Renaissance Dog."

"Yes," replied Olga, rather sappily, "he is."

The next morning, Minerva went to the Animal Shelter, where she spent all day interviewing the cats. She left with a large white Persian named Sigmund, and two black siblings named Carl and Carla.

"You will be founders of the Feline Federation of Therapists," she informed them, after taking them to Fleur de Lily's. "I leave it to you to recruit the other members, and to train them in the various schools of psychotherapy you represent."

"Must we live here?" asked Sigmund, looking around rather disdainfully.

"Not necessarily," smiled Minerva. "Come to think of it, you might like it better across the street with Morgana."

Sigmund twitched his tail noncommittally but – as soon as Minerva left – ambled casually over to Morgana's. By the next day, he was reclining on a huge velvet pillow in the window and being served gourmet cat food.

Carl and Carla stayed at Fleur de Lily's, where – every midnight – the chosen cats gathered for FFT training. Carl told stories of Cat Heroes and Cat Goddesses, and explained how these archetypes determined human behavior. Sigmund often argued with Carl about whether cat-tails were phallic symbols or if female cats suffered from tail-envy. After these esoteric discussions, Carla quietly advocated the advantages of curling up on a lap, purring and listening.

Just before dawn, all the cats went out the alley door and returned to the shops where they had chosen to reside. Each place had at least one resident cat therapist, who was treated with the respect that a long day of purring and sleeping and being petted deserved. It was hard work – but someone had to do it!

Ω Ω Ω

By summertime, everyone declared The Co-op a success. Financially no one was getting rich, but everyone was covering their costs and making enough. Lily and Ophelia were making enough to live on. The Senior Women were making enough so that living on a fixed income was no longer a worry. And though Morgana was making less, it was still more than enough.

Valkira and her friends made very little, but were having so much fun doing it that they did not need more. As was also the case with all the adults participating in The Co-op. The old people shared their wisdom, the young shared their enthusiasm. Each contributed what they were able, all reaped the satisfaction of doing good work together. The old no longer felt useless, the young no longer felt unnecessary. Together they discovered how to enjoy life responsibly.

"I think we should have a Celebration," said Morgana, presiding as usual at the weekly gathering of The Co-op at Fleur de Lily's.

Excited murmuring swept the room as a dozen hands shot up.

"The Chair recognizes Lily." Morgana smiled as she called on her protegée.

"That's a wonderful idea!" said Lily, in a strong confident voice. "We could close off the ends of the street and turn The Co-op into our own mall."

"And we should leave it closed," nodded Eugene. "Bicycles only!"

"Yeah, who needs all those cars whizzing through," agreed C.Chaplin.

"Especially since they don't obey our traffic dogs," added Ventura.

"We'll need to get a permit from the Town Council," objected Ms. Anthony.

"You can do that, can't you?" said Morgana quickly. "All in favor?"

"Aye!" concurred those present.

"We could invite other people who might be interested in joining The Co-op to participate," suggested Carmen.

"Such as?" asked Albert.

"There are some women at the Senior Center who have expressed interest in starting a restaurant here," replied Audrey.

"We can always use good food!" said Theodore eagerly.

"All in favor?"

"Aye!"

"We'll need a decorating committee," said Belle.

"And you're just the person to be in charge," said Morgana. "All in favor?"

"Aye!"

"And we'll need music," said Ophelia, with no trace of her former shyness.

"Are you volunteering?" asked Morgana. "All in favor?"

"Aye!"

And so it went, until everyone – except Morgana – had 'volunteered' for a committee.

"That takes care of just about everything," said Morgana. "But – oh yes – we'll need a clean-up committee."

"Are you volunteering?" piped up Valkira, imitating Morgana to perfection. "All in favor?"

"Aye!" laughed everyone in the room.

Morgana opened her mouth to protest. But smiled instead, and joined the laughter.

Ω Ω Ω

On the day of the Celebration, The Co-op looked as magical as it was. Large whimsical sculptures blocked the ends of the street. Each of several portals was topped with balloons and streamers, welcoming those on foot or riding bikes, but too small for automobiles to pass through. In the middle of the enclosed square was a brightly painted gazebo, flags and pennants fluttering on its roof.

On either side of the gazebo were refreshment stands at which nervous ladies from the Senior Center were selling traditional casseroles and sugar cookies custom-decorated with personalized logos. All of the shops had sidewalk stands exhibiting their best wares, and everyone was wearing the most festive version of their Costumes.

Dogs of the Co-op Canine Corps, wearing new uniforms, proudly patrolled the street. Members of the Feline Federation of Therapists, wearing fancy collars and purring loudly, reclined elegantly on plush pillows in shop windows. Elijah and the football team were giving free rides on their rickshaws. And all the various groups that made music in Ophelia's loft were giving concerts in the gazebo.

Late in the afternoon was the parade. Starting at one portal, circling the gazebo, down to the opposite end, then back, Mr. Marcheson led the Co-op band in bright new uniforms. Each section had designed its own – trumpets in red, trombones in blue, French Horns in purple, piccolos in yellow. Bright plumes and fluttering flags created a brilliant kaleidoscope of color and sound.

Every store had its own float, pulled by Elijah and his team. Albert and his ex-bullies had mounted a miniature windmill on a green field sprouting energy-saving slogans. Carmen and Belle sat beside a giant gilded garbage can spilling over with opulent treasure. Ventura perched atop a large papier-māché globe surrounded by stacks of books. Even the Canine Corps had a cart pulled by Wolf, on which four dogs in uniform sat saluting the CCC flag in the center. Not to be outdone, the FFT's cart was shaped like an analyst's couch, on which Sigmund reclined majestically. Katya and Koshka, both of whom were somewhat enamored of him, sat at his feet. Olga – who had planned to help Wolf with the CCC – was instead pulling the feline float; she had a dark scowl on her face. The two Siamese cats had cleverly appealed to Olga's sense of family duty, harassing her shamelessly until she finally gave in.

After the parade had circled the gazebo several times, Ashley's dance troupe – which had been practicing in Belle's basement – gave a performance. Then Mrs. Price directed Ophelia's chorus in the premiere of the new Co-op Anthem. Everyone joined in the singing and dancing, which continued joyously into the night.

Overhead, fireworks made by Mr. Quark's science class exploded and illuminated the sky.

Meanwhile, on the roof of the old bank, Morgana and Minerva surveyed the festivities with great satisfaction.

"Everyone seems to be having a good time," observed Morgana, leaning back in a leather upholstered chair.

"Yes, they are," replied Minerva, relaxing in the other leather chair on the small penthouse deck. "Are you?"

"I think perhaps I am having the time of my life!" Morgana picked up the champagne flute on the table between the chairs. "This whole Co-op, in fact, is probably the best thing I've ever done."

"It's been profitable?" asked Minerva, picking up her own glass of champagne.

"Surprisingly, yes," replied Morgana. "Oh, less than my usual portfolio, of course – but it's worth every penny I'm not getting!"

"Really?!" Minerva smiled, pleased.

"Making people happy is more satisfying than just making money."

"Especially this kind of happiness," Minerva added. "Everyone down there is celebrating because they've found a way to be useful doing what they enjoy."

"And they are doing it together!" exclaimed Morgana fervently. "No one is lonely anymore."

Both women sipped their champagne, savoring the convivial moment.

One of the science class rockets exploded overhead in a bright shower of multi-colored stars. Valkira and Theodore swooped up after it, inscribing a big loop *à deux*.

"Valkira used to be so lonely." Minerva laughed, as her granddaughter saluted on her way down.

"So did Theodore." Morgana, too, laughed, as he waved one of his wings. "Thank you for helping him."

"Mostly that was Valkira's doing." Minerva gave her a sidelong glance. "You should thank her."

"Yes, I suppose I should." agreed Morgana grudgingly.

"Valkira has no tolerance for what she perceives as injustice and untruthfulness," said Minerva quietly.

"Is that why she goes out of her way to irritate me?"

"Like making you the clean-up committee?"

"I'm not as bad as she thinks," grumbled Morgana.

"Theodore says you got your hands rather dirty fixing this place up," commented Minerva, after a long pause. "Was that so bad?"

"Well, no. Not really." Morgana sighed. "But I'm not looking forward to cleaning up this mess!"

"Well, maybe I can help." Minerva gazed pointedly at Morgana's walking stick, which was resting against her chair. Suddenly the $ sign on its silver globe started blinking excitedly. Minerva picked it up and pointed at an overflowing garbage can next to one of the Senior Ladies' refreshment stands.

ZAP! The can was empty.

"Here, try this." Minerva handed it, still blinking, to Morgana.

She, in turn, pointed at another bulging trash receptacle.

POW! That, too, miraculously vanished.

A huge grin covered Morgana's face, as she reached for the bottle in the champagne bucket. "Here's to our wonderful grandchildren!" she exclaimed, filling their glasses.

"Both of them!" added Minerva, also smiling hugely.

"But don't tell Valkira about this!" laughed Morgana, nodding toward her walking stick.

The two grandmothers drained their glasses and threw them at the chimney. Then they both roared with laughter.

And when, at last, they settled back in their chairs, Minerva discovered that her own irritation with Morgana had dissolved.

Chapter 11

The Campaign

It was the last week of summer vacation. The Co-op had hummed with convivial creativity during all the busy months of no school. Now, however, the young members would soon have to return to the confines of Jane Addams Junior High. None of them were pleased at the prospect.

Valkira and Theodore had spent the morning in Ophelia's loft, playing oboe-bassoon duets. Having made rapid progress in her piano lessons with Mrs. Price, Ophelia was accompanying them.

Taking a break, the three friends relaxed on the comfortable cushions strewn about the floor.

"I can't believe summer is almost over," sighed Theodore. "I'm not ready to go back."

"I will never be ready!" said Valkira vehemently. "It's so boring!"

"But at least no one picks on us anymore," commented Ophelia, always trying to see the bright side.

"True," agreed Theodore, "but wouldn't it be wonderful if we could do there what we do here?!"

"Like we did before the School Board banned Celebrations," said Ophelia. "If only we could make them change their mind."

"Maybe we can," Valkira sat up straight, as an idea struck her, "if someone from The Co-op gets on the School Board!"

Just then, Ms. Anthony walked in the door of Fleur de Lily's. After exchanging polite howls of greeting with Wolf, she ascended the stairs to the Costume workshop, where she delivered some books Lily had requested. On her way out, she stopped to chat with her students.

"I can't believe school is starting this year without me," she said sadly, sitting down on a vacant cushion.

"Just be glad you don't have to be there," said Valkira, surprised that Ms. Anthony did not appreciate her good fortune.

"But what will I do all day while you are all there?" lamented Ms. Anthony. "How can I be a teacher without students?"

"Maybe you need to start teaching our parents," suggested Theodore, "what real education is about."

"Why don't you run for the School Board?!" exclaimed Valkira. "You could convince them to let the school be a good place again!"

"Hmmm. That's not a bad idea." Ms. Anthony's eyes lit up, as she considered. "I think I would enjoy the challenge – and could do the job right. But it takes a lot of money to get elected to anything these days."

"Well, maybe that needs to change!" argued Valkira. "Surely there's another way to run for office! After all, we're supposed to be a democracy, right?!"

"Sometimes Money makes people forget that," Ms. Anthony frowned. "But it would be an interesting learning project to see if one could get elected without spending any."

"Let's bring it up at the next Co-op meeting," suggested Theodore enthusiastically.

"Good idea!" Ms. Anthony stood up excitedly. "Meanwhile, I shall talk to the Co-op grandmothers."

To no one's surprise, The Co-op ringingly endorsed Ms. Anthony's candidacy for the School Board. And everyone volunteered for The Campaign. As did most of the teachers at

Jane Addams Junior High. Ms. Anthony's platform advocated restoring the Celebrations and reinstating Music and Foreign Languages to the curriculum. In the weeks leading up to the election, all members of The Co-op spoke earnestly to family, friends and neighbors about the benefits of these programs, as well as Ms. Anthony's undeniable dedication to the cause of quality education. Many of the incumbents, however, dismissed her candidacy as inconsequential.

They were shocked when Ms. Anthony won a seat on The Board. And by a rather substantial margin.

The Co-op celebrated.

Ms. Anthony took her victory as a mandate for change, and got immediately to work implementing her campaign promises.

Restoring the Celebrations was the easiest. Especially after the teachers testified that State Test scores had gone up afterward, but dropped following their abolition. Then, too, even opponents had found the Celebrations entertaining.

Reinstating Music and Foreign Languages was not objected to in principle, but when discussing how to re-fund these programs, The Board was sharply divided. Ms. Anthony suggested taking money from the over-endowed Competitive Sports budget, and dividing it equally among all school programs. After a bitterly acrimonious debate, the proposal narrowly passed.

The Co-op again celebrated.

The Opposition, however, was furious, and began to coalesce. The town jocks were incensed by the perceived threat to town manhood, and the possible loss of entertainment provided by athletic games. The Patriotic Legion wondered if the alleged attack on football was an un-American activity; it was even rumored that Ms. Anthony was a Communist! And behind all this, those associated with The Store worried that The Co-op might be undercutting their profits.

The Town Council, of course, was controlled by The Opposition. Soon, taxes on Co-op businesses were significantly increased. City Inspectors suddenly swarmed all over its buildings, levying outrageous fines for miniscule infractions. The permit to block off The Co-op's main street was revoked, and the speed limit was raised.

As The Town polarized, the stream of visitors to The Co-op decreased and business declined. The morale of its proprietors plummeted accordingly.

Deeply concerned, Minerva paid a visit to Morgana's bank.

"For the first time," said Morgana, sitting in her office, "my investments in The Co-op are showing a loss."

"Isn't that just part of a normal business cycle?" asked Minerva, with just a trace of sarcasm.

"For normal business, yes," replied Morgana, frowning. "But The Co-op isn't a normal business. It's much more!"

"Even to you?"

"Especially to me!" declared Morgana emphatically.

"Then we are agreed that something must be done to stop those who are trying to destroy it?"

"Absolutely!" exclaimed Morgana, loudly thumping J.P.'s walking stick on the floor.

Seeing the steely glint in Morgana's eyes, Minerva was very glad they were on the same side.

Ω Ω Ω

A special meeting of The Co-op was called the following weekend. As members gathered in Fleur de Lily's, anger was running high.

"We all know why we're here," said Morgana, calling the meeting to order. "The Co-op is under attack by people who feel threatened by what we are doing. We need to protect ourselves!"

"But what we do hurts no one and benefits many!" protested Belle, swishing her tutu irately.

"Unfortunately, not everyone sees that," replied Carmen, with an angry click of her castanets.

"Then we must explain it to them!" Ventura crossed her arms purposefully over her silver-studded leather vest.

"Some people won't believe us," cautioned Minerva. "Especially those with power."

"Why not?" asked Audrey, peering over her large rhinestone-trimmed sunglasses.

"Because they're afraid of losing that power!" exclaimed Carmen, stomping her boot-taps.

"Then we must get some power, too!" said Minerva.

"How?" asked Lily, in her assertive new voice.

"We got Ms. Anthony onto the School Board," replied Minerva. "Let's elect one of us to be Mayor!"

Everyone cheered.

"That's a great idea, Grandmère!" shouted Valkira. "I nominate you!"

"No, no, I'm much too – different – to get anyone's vote."

In reluctant agreement, everyone nodded .

"But you're not, Gran!" yelled Theodore. "You're almost as conservative as the people in power! But you're smart – and honest. And I think you'd make a great Mayor!"

Hear! Hear!

"But there's never been a senior woman mayor in this town!" protested Morgana.

"So what!" shouted Ventura. "It's high time!"

Amidst enthusiastic cheers, Morgana was unanimously acclaimed The Co-op's candidate for Mayor.

As the hurrahs continued, Morgana's look of surprise transformed into an enormously pleased grin. Elated, she broke into uncharacteristic song. "I am Woman," she belted out, doffing her J.P. hat and flourishing the walking stick. "Hear me roar!"

Ω Ω Ω

The Campaign Committee, consisting of Carmen and Belle, Audrey and Ventura, took charge. Starting with the widows at their condo, they began organizing a quietly effective network which eventually reached into almost every corner of town.

Each of them gave several coffee parties, to which they invited small cliques of old women. There, it was explained why Morgana was running for Mayor, and what she promised to do if elected. Each woman was asked to spread the word by discussing it with their families, and by inviting Morgana to speak at the various community groups of which they were members.

The Co-op's Platform was clear and straightforward: Fair Taxes, Fair Laws, Fairly Enforced. The network grew rapidly. A steady stream of Letters-to-the-Editor flooded the Media; invitations for Morgana to speak proliferated. For predominantly male groups, she emphasized Free Enterprise and More Jobs; with women's groups, she stressed Quality Education. As The Campaign progressed, Morgana honed her public speaking skills and began to take pride in the persuasiveness of her speeches.

Meanwhile, on the home front, the town grandmothers were also persuasive. They urged their sons to ensure a level playing field for Morgana's candidacy and allow fair discussion of issues raised. They exhorted their daughters to stand solidly behind the wise woman advocating better education. Some also encouraged – albeit tacitly – wives to influence husbands by various traditional means. In many households, men were suddenly overwhelmed by steady diets of favorite meals. Or noticed a singular lack thereof – depending. And as the election approached, some wives started having headaches which lasted for days. Or the opposite – again depending. Word of such tactics, of course, was carefully prevented from getting back to Minerva.

The grandchildren also campaigned actively. They created media events with concerts in the Co-op gazebo. They made posters and wore T-shirts that said "Morgana for Mayor = Fair

Government." The band concluded each half-time show at football games by spelling out "M for M."

And, most importantly, the teenagers at Jane Addams Junior High talked – really talked – to their parents. About how much more they were learning because of Ms. Anthony's reforms, about how much less trouble they were getting into because of The Co-op. And they did so without teenage jargon – and no attitude. Parents, in turn, were speechless with amazement.

While grandmothers and grandchildren industriously campaigned for Morgana's election, The Establishment officially refused to take her candidacy seriously. Privately, however, they decided not to repeat their previous error of underestimating Ms. Anthony's electability. Though not all the town fathers disagreed that political change was overdue, much behind-the-scenes pressure was nonetheless exerted on all the menfolk to stay loyal to the pack.

On election day, the condo grandmothers made sure all senior citizens whose drivers' licenses had been revoked had rides to the Polls. Likewise, the Senior Center set up a babysitting service so that mothers of young children could vote. Women, in general, turned out in record numbers. Many men, in hopes of decent meals and no headaches – without censure from male peers – conveniently "forgot" to vote.

As the votes were counted that evening, the election was – for several hours – too close to call. Finally, Morgana was proclaimed the winner – and by a large enough margin to claim Victory.

Large crowds of grandmothers and grandchildren converged on The Co-op and jubilantly celebrated.

Meanwhile, small groups of outraged men gathered sullenly at various watering holes around town.

Ω Ω Ω

Much later that night, after everyone had gone home, Morgana retired to the small apartment above The Co-op bank. She had installed it for times – like this – when it was too late to drive back to her condo.

Excited as she was, sleep did not come. Restlessly, she went up to the rooftop deck and gazed happily at the stars. Lost in a reverie of how she would redecorate the Mayor's office – literally and figuratively – she did not notice the distant sound of approaching engines. By the time they burst into the street below, it was too late to do anything but stare in horror.

Dozens of motorcycles, revving raucously, roared up and down the street, their riders whooping like barbarians. All of them wore cowboy hats and kerchiefs masking their faces. Most were waving baseball bats; a few brandished rifles. Smashing windows and breaking down doors, they rode into Co-op shops, demolishing everything in sight.

The Canine Corps defended their territory valiantly. Wolf led repeated charges, growling ferociously. The dogs, however, were greatly outnumbered – and outgunned. Bats were swung and shots fired; painful yelps mingled sickeningly with the sound of breaking glass and roaring engines.

Through tear-filled eyes, Morgana watched, paralyzed, as the marauders circled the gazebo. Some of them jumped off their motorcycles, erected a huge dollar sign on top, and set fire to it. As it blazed, the vigilantes revved their engines and hooted drunkenly.

Ω Ω Ω

Dawn broke slowly; Morgana's sobs subsided. The Posse had finally departed, leaving the gazebo in ashes and all the shops ravaged.

Cautiously, she went down into the street, where she was joined by Lily and Ophelia. Injured dogs lay everywhere, a few already dead. The local veterinarian – summoned by Lily – arrived and immediately went to work, cursing under his breath at the barbarous treatment of the animals. Searching frantically, Ophelia finally found Wolf, grievously wounded, behind a pile of shattered glass. Tears poured from her eyes as she sobbed his name, desperately trying to staunch his bleeding. Wolf looked up weakly from still loyal eyes, pleading forgiveness for having failed her.

The sun had fully risen by the time all the dogs had been tended. Many were taken to the hospital; others hobbled painfully or lay miserably on cushions salvaged from the wreckage. Ophelia had gone with Wolf – in critical condition – to the intensive care unit.

As members of The Co-op returned to the place where they had so recently celebrated victory, shock and dismay echoed up and down the street. Minerva was the last to arrive. White-faced, she stood on the steps of the gazebo's charred skeleton, regarding all the havoc surrounding her. Heartsick, she nonetheless braced herself, knowing that this was no time to fall apart.

Instead, she busied herself encouraging weeping friends, organizing clean-up crews, and planning a memorial service for the brave dogs fallen in battle. Olga, meanwhile, hastened to Wolf's bedside.

By evening, the worst of the debris had been collected in dumpsters, and the extent of the damage ascertained. It would take weeks before The Co-op was back in business. Even after Morgana offered interest-free loans to cover the cost of repair, everyone was discouraged.

A pyre was erected on the remains of the gazebo. As the dogs were given a hero's farewell, all members of The Co-op wept copiously. Not just for the canine friends who had so courageously sacrificed themselves, but for the hope of a better day which seemed to be going up in flames with them.

As Minerva stood watching, she was consumed with furious déjà vu.

Ω Ω Ω

As soon as Wolf was pronounced out of danger, Olga and Minerva flew to The Sanctuary. Olga landed in the parking lot next to the Troika. Dog and horses were soon noisily commiserating in mournful Russian.

Relieved that her message had been received, Minerva hurried into the castle coffeehouse and sat down at the center table across from Babushka Ekaterina.

"It's happening again," said Minerva, trying to keep her voice steady.

"Yes, I know," replied Babushka Ekaterina, her wise old eyes looking deep into Minerva's soul.

"I thought we could change things . . . ." Minerva's tears spilled over.

"And we are, we are." She grasped Minerva's hands. "But these things take time."

"But no matter <u>what</u> we do, no matter how hard we work to protect our children . . . . <u>They</u> are always out there – breaking everything that means anything."

"It's been that way for a long, long time," said Babushka Ekaterina sadly.

"Why can't they stop? Why can't we <u>make</u> them stop?!" exclaimed Minerva, angrily wiping her tears.

"Maybe – to do that – we need help."

"From whom?" Minerva lowered her handkerchief.

"From the Grandfathers," replied Babushka Ekaterina quietly.

Chapter 12

Grandpère

Bentley got up early and walked out to the balcony of his comfortable chateau. It was halfway up a hill overlooking the main meeting area of The Retreat, and provided an excellent view of the valley and other dwellings dotting its surrounding hills. All of the buildings were nestled among ancient trees which soared up to the sky like pillars of a huge cathedral. Several thousand acres of this prime timber had been donated by one of The Retreat's founders, a wealthy lumber baron who had made his millions by chopping down all the other big trees in the area. Bentley considered him a great man for preserving this natural treasure for the enjoyment of people who deserved it.

The Retreat was – of course – private, a place where members of The Club could get away from the rigors of manipulating Money. Power was a heavy burden, and the unsung heroes who carried it needed relaxation. They were, after all, the Best People, untainted by inferior races and religions, who nobly protected the weak women and children never allowed inside The Retreat.

Bentley himself had retired from The City some years ago. Instead of spending only occasional weekends at The Retreat, like his son did, he now lived here permanently. Only rarely did he leave it for infrequent visits to The Club. Like other retired members, Bentley took his duties as Club Conservator very seriously. Among other things, they administered The Club dues, which were high enough to keep out undesirables.

Tonight was the opening ceremony of the yearly Midsummer Gathering, at which members from all corners of the Earth congregated. Many of them brought guests, usually up-and-coming movers-and-shakers to be vetted as future members. Since The Patricians considered it *noblesse oblige* to patronize the Arts, several famous performers were also invited. Unlike the kitchen help, they were allowed to enter at the front gate. But though they were invited to all the festivities, they were expected to sing – often – for their supper.

From his balcony, Bentley saw a steady stream of limousines arriving just inside the gate, discharging exalted passengers, then departing to the outside world. He dressed quickly and walked down to welcome his heroes and toast – very liberally – their arrival.

Later, he walked – a little unsteadily – back to his chateau and put on his robe. The Ceremony traditionally opened with a rousing rendition of The Anthem sung by The Choir. Bentley was a member and dressed carefully in his custom-tailored linen toga. He was fortunately tall and, sucking in his gut, looked almost noble – unlike some in the choir who were rather portly. And had less hair. Bentley's was still thick enough to look Roman without a comb-over. Some of the others were struggling with that. Time for a toupée? No, that wasn't done. Most choir members resigned instead. Bentley congratulated himself that he would be singing for several more years. And that his not entirely gray hair made him look distinguished.

The Club members and guests were seated in an open amphitheatre carved into the hill. The stage was bordered by several trees, carved into rustic Greek columns. After the Honorary High Priest invoked the Gods – who were, of course, on their side – he led The Patricians in The Oath of Secrecy and Brotherhood. As Bentley proudly marched onto the platform with The Choir, he felt like Julius Caesar marching into Gaul with his legions. None of those assembled noticed the bulging bellies under the togas, or the balding comb-overs, or that the choir sang off-key. They were The Patricians, The Best People, The Chosen Men – whatever they did was Right and Perfect.

After Bentley and The Choir left the stage, one of the guests sang a favorite operatic aria about fickle women. He was a famous Tenor from the City Opera. His singing was right on key and perfect. The members applauded enthusiastically. If they had the time, they knew they could do that, too. Because they were The Best People.

After several other command performances by imported artists, The Ceremony closed with the traditional act by new members. As the older members whistled and cheered, the middle-aged men trotted coyly onto the stage dressed as women. Their performance of "There is Nothing like a Dame" – complete with waggling fannies and huge false boobs – brought down the house.

The next day, Bentley slept late and arose reluctantly, mightily hungover. Nonetheless he attended the daily talk in the Discussion Place always given by an Important Person. Today's speaker was a member of The Cabinet, holding forth on a proposed law to strengthen Family Values. Among other things, it included a plan to outlaw the recent activities of the grandmothers. Everyone in the group was as hungover as Bentley, but like him, were pretending not to be. A Patrician, after all, was expected to hold his liquor like a man.

Just as Bentley – despite his best efforts – was dozing off, a gasp of disbelief woke everyone up. Bentley jerked his eyes open and, with the startled others, looked up. And there in the sky, he beheld a most horrifying sight.

Olga and the sled were making glittering loops around the group. Then, circling in so low that the Important Person had to duck, she landed nearby. Minerva descended majestically from the silver sled, recently polished for the occasion, and sat down in the front row.

"I'm here to discuss Family Values," she remarked casually.

Bentley slunk out of the Discussion Place, and fled to his chateau as fast as his hangover allowed. Out of the corner of her eye, Minerva saw him go.

She was waiting for him on the balcony.

"So," she said, as Bentley fell into his chair, "this is where you've been hiding all these years."

"What are you doing here?!" croaked Bentley.

"We need to talk," replied Minerva.

"But not here!"

"Where else? You haven't left this place in years!"

"This is where My Work is!" protested Bentley, recovering his dignity.

"What work?! Drinking with all these old geezers?!"

"How dare you call them that!" Bentley was indignant. "They are the Best People!!"

"Then why don't they act like it?!"

Both of them were silent, biting back angry retorts too often exchanged in the past.

"Why are you here?" Bentley finally asked quietly.

"Your granddaughter needs your help," replied Minerva, also quietly.

"My granddaughter?" He was startled. "But I don't even know her."

"It's time you met her." Minerva's eyes softened. "She's a wonderful child."

"But she can't come here," said Bentley nervously.

"Then I'll take you to her."

Bentley was silent. "Well, I don't know . . . ."

"I'll come get you next week. If you don't come with me, I promise I will return with some of my friends. And we will give your Best People quite a show."

Bentley blanched.

Minerva stepped back into her sled. "And you should see what they fly!" Olga took off, dodging skillfully between the big trees.

As the sled disappeared, Bentley breathed a huge sigh of relief. And then became extremely vexed.

THAT WOMAN! Why did she have to be so difficult?! Why couldn't she understand what was important?! Why did she insist on telling him things he didn't want to hear?! Why did she blame him for what wasn't his fault?!

And she actually expected him to leave The Retreat to meet a child?! A girl?! Why was she trying to dredge up the past?!

Painful memories suddenly menaced, lurking in the corner of his mind. Bentley skillfully banished them, as he had been doing for so many years.

Still, he did not wish to be embarrassed in front of the Best People.

And Minerva always kept her word.

Ω Ω Ω

After school, Valkira ran all the way to Minerva's house. She had been invited to The Sanctuary, and was very excited about her first ride in the silver sled. "I've always wondered where you went when you flew over the birch trees."

"And now you will see for yourself," said Minerva, pleased by Valkira's eagerness. "There are some people who want to meet you."

As Olga soared into the air, Valkira gripped the sides of the sled and held on tight – especially when Olga could not resist making an ostentatious loop right over Jane Addams Junior High.

"Don't be a show-off, Olga!" warned Minerva. "This is Valkira's first flight."

Olga looked chastened, and slowed down. There were no more loops.

As they approached The Sanctuary, Valkira peered cautiously over the side – and exclaimed delightedly at what she saw below. The old amusement park was ringed by a thick fence dingy enough to make the place appear abandoned – and uninteresting. It was also high enough to discourage the unwelcome. Within the walls, however, the old park had been cleverly recycled into a beautiful village. Around the castle were several comfortable cottages, surrounded by green gardens dotted with picturesque ponds. Just inside the high fence, tall trees bordered the park; shade trees were strategically placed near brightly-painted benches from dismantled carnival rides. Tracks from the roller coaster had been converted into a miniature railroad which connected the buildings; oddly-shaped vehicles moved purposefully from place to place. The carousel had become the central diner for residents of the village; the ferris wheel had been converted into a giant windmill.

Olga landed extra carefully, and pulled up next to Babushka Ekaterina's Troika. Minerva took Valkira's hand, led her to the castle, and into the circular coffeehouse.

Valkira stopped, speechless, trying to take it all in. "This is the most wonderful place I've ever been!" she finally exclaimed.

Minerva took her to the center table, and introduced her. "Valkira, these are my best friends. They are eager to be yours, too."

"Welcome! Welcome!" beamed Babushka Ekaterina. She was echoed by all the others, each in her own language, all of which Valkira had no trouble understanding. And soon she was benevolently enveloped by the complete attention of the International Corps of Grandmothers.

Knowing that Valkira was in the best of all possible hands, Minerva returned to the sled. There was someone else who needed to meet her granddaughter.

Ω Ω Ω

Olga flew quickly to The Retreat, and landed quietly on the balcony of Bentley's chateau.

He was ready and waiting. As Minerva thought he probably would be. To be embarrassed in front of the Best People – for him, that was a fate worse than death.

"Do you expect me to ride in that thing?" he asked irritably.

"If you'd rather, we could fly in Sophia's Chariot," replied Minerva sarcastically. "But Olga is a much better pilot than her ugly old camel."

"Oh, all right," grumbled Bentley, as he climbed awkwardly into the sled. "Let's get this over with."

Olga took off none too gently, and dodged the trees rather more abruptly than was necessary. And just as she cleared the top of the biggest tree, she made a giant loop. Bentley tried unsuccessfully to hide his queasiness.

As they approached The Sanctuary, curiosity overcame airsickness; he stared, amazed, at the odd-looking compound toward which they were heading. Olga landed with a bump, and Bentley climbed unsteadily out of the sled. As Minerva led him to the carousel diner, he looked around disdainfully – but definitely intrigued.

"We believe in recycling," commented Minerva, reading his look.

Entering the diner, Minerva left him at a booth of facing carousel benches. Then she went to get her granddaughter.

At the castle coffeehouse, Valkira was having the time of her life, basking in the center of several doting grandmothers. Never had Minerva seen her so animated and so bright and so witty. And rarely had she seen her friends so delighted, and having such a good time.

She swelled with pride. What a wonderful child! And how wonderful that her friends appreciated that, too! Only with difficulty was Minerva able to extract Valkira from the circle of adoring grandmothers.

"Grandmère, your friends are just great!" chattered Valkira excitedly. "And this is such a cool place! Can I come back?"

"Of course! I think my friends would be disappointed if you didn't," replied Minerva, as they walked toward the carousel. "But now there is someone else you must see – someone you've been wanting to meet for a long time."

Entering the carousel, she took Valkira to the booth where Bentley was sitting. "Valkira," she said quietly, "this is your grandfather."

Valkira stood, astonished, looking at the man about whom she had so often asked her grandmother – who had always evaded her questions.

Bentley, too, was stunned. She looked so much like someone else . . . . someone he had tried so hard to forget, someone about whom he had always evaded thinking.

"Sit down, dear." Minerva indicated the bench opposite Bentley, and then went to the coffee bar in the center and ordered a latte. Climbing on a carousel horse turned barstool, she waited, just out of earshot, keeping watch in the reflection of the mosaic carousel mirrors.

"You look like my Dad – sort of," said Valkira, breaking the charged silence. "Is this what he'll look like, when he's old?"

"Probably," replied Bentley. "He looks a lot like I did when I was his age."

"So you've seen him?"

"Why, yes, I see him occasionally," smiled Bentley. "At The Club."

"Is that the place in The City that doesn't let girls in?"

"Well – um – er – yes." Bentley squirmed a little. "Yes, that's the one."

"Why not?" asked Valkira, as always, direct.

"Well – ah – because we talk about important business there." Bentley was starting to feel uncomfortable, an unpleasant sensation from which living at The Retreat usually spared him.

"What kind of business?" persisted Valkira. "Is it a secret?"

"Well, no, not exactly. But you have to be a grown-up to understand it."

"But Grandmère is a grown-up," protested Valkira. "And Dad got really mad when she went there to talk to him about business."

"Well – um – women aren't supposed to be there, either." Picturing Minerva at The Club made Bentley nervous.

"Why not?" Valkira's direct gaze was unfaltering. "Is The Club afraid of women?"

Bentley dropped his eyes. *What an insufferable child! She's just like her grandmother!*

Finally, he cleared his throat and began again. "Your grandmother tells me you're very bright."

"Yes, I am," said Valkira, with her usual matter-of-fact forthrightness. "I'm the only 10-year-old at Jane Addams Junior High.

"That must be fun," commented Bentley inanely.

"No, it's not," said Valkira. "Most of the time it's lonely."

Silence.

"Where have you been?" asked Valkira abruptly.

"Excuse me?" Bentley was startled.

"All this time, where have you been?" repeated Valkira. "You've visited Dad – why haven't I ever met you?"

"Well – um – I've been busy."

"Doing what?" insisted Valkira.

"Well – um – doing all the things men have to do to protect their families."

"From what?"

"Well – um – it's a dangerous world out there . . . ."

"Because angry men keep breaking things we work so hard to build?" Valkira's utterly honest eyes blazed at him.

Bentley was sweating. *If only she wouldn't look at me that way! If only she didn't look so much like . . . .*

"Who is going to protect us from that?!" demanded Valkira.

The unanswered question echoed around the carousel.

Chapter 13

The Retreat

It had been the second worst day of Bentley's life.

After the unpleasant interview with his granddaughter, Minerva put Bentley on the sled – solo – and directed Olga to return him to The Retreat.

Olga flew with a vengeance, her normally happy husky face shooting back frequent dirty looks. Not wishing to damage the sled, she pulled up to his balcony just short of a crash landing.

Bentley extricated himself unsteadily and collapsed in his chair.

"ГрррЛ!" Olga scowled darkly. Then she took off, flying low – and ostentatiously – over every corner of The Retreat.

Imploring the God he rarely thought about to let all the Best People be too inebriated to look up, Bentley reached for the almost full bottle of Scotch always at his elbow.

By the time the bottle was empty, he had drunk himself into oblivion. Which was what he always did when confronted with the painful memories.

Ω Ω Ω

The next morning, Bentley had an acute – but very peculiar – hangover. The nausea was as unpleasant as ever, but this time there was no compensating loss of memory. Everything about the previous day was absolutely clear in his mind. When his headache finally subsided, and he reached for another bottle, yesterday's events were illuminated by an almost blinding light.

Bentley sat back, looking up at the trees, until the sun was setting. Reaching – from habit – for the drink in front of him, his hand hesitated.

No. Not this time. I can't hide in there any longer.

And, at last, allowed himself to remember.

And then he fell peacefully asleep, untroubled by the painful nightmares which had too often invaded his dreams.

The next day, Bentley awakened refreshed – and more alert than he had felt in years. Suddenly everything made sense.

Minerva was right. He had been hiding.

Alexander had been his first-born, his pride and joy. Brilliant and talented, handsome and charming, Bentley had lovingly groomed him to follow in his footsteps. But after graduating from The University (with Honors, of course), Alex had been drafted. Following basic training, he was to be shipped around the world to fight in a country no one had ever heard of for a cause no one quite understood.

Alex had serious reservations about the rectitude of The Conflict, and looked to his parents for guidance.

Bentley and Minerva, however, argued constantly about what to do. She insisted that Alex should go to The North until The Conflict was over. He, however, having fought in the Great War, thought that his son also had a duty to defend his country.

"But is this really defending our country?!" Minerva had asked in despair.

Bentley himself also had doubts. But The Patricians all insisted that, of course, this was any real man's patriotic duty.

And, since they were the Best People, they must be right. Anyone who was Anyone had to believe that.

And so, he had sent his beloved son off to war.

A year later, Alex returned – in a body bag – with a posthumous medal for bravery.

Minerva had wept and raged – and thrown the medal in her husband's face.

Bentley, struggling to restrain his own angry tears, rescued the medal. Respectfully he had put it back in its case – and buried it where he would never have to see it again.

The Patricians, of course, congratulated him on his son's brave sacrifice. "It's what the Best Men do," they insisted.

Desperately, Bentley tried to believe them. Something being with Minerva would not let him do. And the sight of Harold, his younger and less gifted son, filled him with guilty anger. *Why couldn't it have been YOU instead!*

And so, unable to face the blame in his wife's eyes, unable to risk loving his other son, unable to cope with the magnitude of his loss, he had left. And, unable to reconcile the ambivalence of the tragedy, Bentley had been hiding all these years in The Retreat, trying to convince himself of the collective superiority of the Best People.

And then he had met Valkira, the very image of his slain son. And remembered how bright and brave and beautiful he had been at that age.

And then, finally, he wept – tears he should have shed years ago.

The following day, he very much wanted to reach for the ubiquitous bottle. Instead, he thought long and hard about what – if anything – he could do to redeem himself.

Finally, he called a meeting at the Discussion Place. The Midsummer Gathering was over; non-resident members and their guests had departed. Only those who lived in The Retreat year-round remained; like Bentley, they were all retired – and grandfathers. And like him, they had all fought in the Great War.

Bentley stood up and cleared his throat nervously. Then took the plunge, and got right to the point.

"Because we are men, we have Power and the Privileges that accompany it. In return, we are supposed to run things for the good of everyone."

"Well, of course," harrumphed a very bald Patrician who had finally quit the choir last year. "That's how God intended it."

"Maybe so," continued Bentley. "But if that's true, we have an obligation to keep our end of the bargain."

"Well, of course," agreed the Bald One. "So what's the problem?"

"The problem is that women and children often need to be protected from what men do in the name of protecting them. Too often, we go to war for all the wrong reasons."

"That's ridiculous! God is always on our side!" protested the Bald One vociferously. "That's why I fought in the Great War."

"So did I. But I don't think that's necessarily true of all our wars since then."

"That's treason!" retorted the Bald One. "My country, right or wrong!" Several others shouted their agreement.

"Not if it puts our sons in harm's way for no good reason!" shouted Bentley over the brouhaha. "Surely there must be a better way! Surely there is some way we can use our Power to <u>help</u> those we love!"

For the first time in years, there was actually discussion in the Discussion Place. It lasted all day, and almost came to blows. Finally, most of the Patrician grandfathers stomped off.

About a dozen remained. They, too, mourned cherished sons, lost in needless battles. And had found the courage to remember.

"All right, then," said Bentley. "Let's see what we can do."

Ω Ω Ω

Minerva was not entirely surprised when Bentley showed up at her door.

"I was hoping you would come," she smiled, glancing at the car parked in front. "I see you decided to drive."

"Flying has never agreed with me," grinned Bentley sheepishly.

"Don't worry. Olga is in the backyard."

"I don't think she's too fond of me."

"Olga is Russian," replied Minerva, raising an eyebrow. "She understands the importance of true friendship and loyalty."

"Something that I am hoping to develop – albeit belatedly."

Minerva nodded, hopeful but skeptical. She sat down next to him on the divan, but kept a careful distance between them.

"You were right. About everything. And I'm sorry. Truly," said Bentley, getting it over with and looking her straight in the eye with more than a little trepidation. "I don't know what else to say."

"Well," said Minerva, surprised but still skeptical, "maybe you need to tell me what you plan to do about it."

"Yes, of course." He cleared his throat purposefully. "Yesterday, we had a meeting –"

"Who is 'we'?" interrupted Minerva.

"Some of the other grandfathers at The Retreat."

"Who have been hiding there, too?"

"Well . . . . yes . . . ."

Minerva was about to inquire as to the cause of this sudden epiphany – then wisely decided not to push her luck. "Go on."

"At our meeting, we decided to use our Power as Patricians to make things better."

"How?"

"First of all, we're going to use our stock portfolios for leverage. We'll buy into Socially Responsible companies, but we're not going to picket the Big Corporations like you've been doing."

"Why not?"

"Because we don't need to. All the CEOs are members of The Club. We'll work from inside the Establishment instead."

"That's a good idea," said Minerva, pleased with his effort. "And it's a good start. But I think the problem goes beyond Money, powerful though that is."

"I fear you're probably right about that," agreed Bentley sadly. "Attitudes – about too many important things – are all twisted up. But we're going to try to change that – starting with our sons."

"Harold? I don't know if there's much hope for him."

"What about Bradford?"

"Maybe. If you can catch him when he's not throwing a ball around."

"Oh now, Minerva," chuckled Bentley, "sports aren't as bad as you think."

"It's not athletics *per se* that I object to," retorted Minerva. "It's how much they displace other important things."

"Yes, that's true," agreed Bentley. "I sometimes wish I'd stayed with the cello instead of going out for football. My knees would certainly be in better shape."

"So why didn't you?"

"My father convinced me that football was the manly thing to do."

" 'The sins of the fathers' . . . ." murmured Minerva. "Surely it's time to break the cycle."

"Indeed," Bentley concurred. "But we need to start when they're young."

"Valkira has a young friend who could use a grandfather," suggested Minerva. "He's a wonderful boy who has been helping her humanize their school."

"I'd like to meet him. And see Valkira again. I don't think I made a very good impression last time."

"You didn't," agreed Minerva. "Fortunately, she is a tolerant – and forgiving – child."

"So you'll arrange it?"

"Yes," promised Minerva, "I will. Come back next Friday."

At the door, Bentley held out his hand. "Minerva – all these years – I've really missed you."

Minerva took his extended hand and pressed it gently. "I've missed you, too."

Impulsively she leaned over and quickly kissed his cheek.

Ω Ω Ω

On the appointed day, Bentley arrived early. Valkira was already waiting for him, sitting on the cats' divan. He sat down next to her – but not too close. Katya strolled over, sniffed him carefully, then sat – ears alert – halfway between grandfather and granddaughter.

"I guess she doesn't distrust me as much as Olga does," began Bentley.

"She's French," observed Valkira cautiously. "She wouldn't be so obvious about it."

"Valkira – I'm sorry I stayed away so long. I would truly like to know you, if you'll let me."

"Why did you? Stay away, I mean."

"Because I was hiding from things I didn't want to remember."

"And that's changed?"

"I hope so. It's very difficult not to be truthful around someone like you." *What a wonderful child! She's just like her grandmother!*

"Grandmère says you want to help," said Valkira, "and that you need a grandson."

"That's true. But first, do I have a granddaughter?" Bentley held out his hand. "I'll try if you will."

Valkira smiled, and they shook hands on it.

The doorbell rang. Minerva answered it and came back with Theodore, who sat down on a chair across from the sofa.

"I hear you've been helping Valkira make your school a good place to learn," said Bentley respectfully, smiling at the boy.

"Yes Sir, we've been trying our best," replied Theodore, not used to having a grown-up male address him as if he mattered. "But it's not easy."

"No, I don't suppose it is," Bentley observed sympathetically. "Is there any way I could help?"

"Oh yes Sir, I think you could!" replied Theodore eagerly. "What do you think, Valkira?"

"I think there's lots he could do," agreed Valkira, and then grinned mischievously. "But first, I think he needs a Costume!"

"A-hah, yes!" laughed Minerva, "Yes! A Costume!"

Theodore hunted for the colored pencils while Valkira handed her grandfather several sheets of paper. "We all have one," she explained excitedly. "It helps us be who we really are – and lets other people see our strength."

"Oh yes, now I remember . . . ." Bentley got a faraway look in his eyes. "Your grandmother used to have some magnificent Costumes . . . ."

"But now you need one," interrupted Minerva, blushing.

Valkira and Theodore grinned at each other, and got to work.

Bentley's Costume was a group effort. "He's been hiding from himself so long, he needs help remembering who he is," said Minerva, directing everyone to make sketches of who they thought he should be.

Bentley regarded each of the drawings carefully, crossing out or circling as he sorted through them. Finally he incorporated bits and pieces into a total ensemble – then showed it to the children, who thought it was wonderful.

Then he handed it to Minerva.

Valkira watched, astounded, as her grandmother laughed – then cried – and then threw her arms around him.

Ω Ω Ω

Minerva and Valkira made a shopping list for what was needed to make Bentley's Costume.

"You can come along, if you'd like," said Minerva as she was walking out to the porch.

"Ярррф!" barked Olga from the backyard.

"No thanks," said Bentley hastily. "I think I'll wait here."

"I'll keep you company," said Theodore.

Valkira grinned and followed her grandmother to the waiting sled.

After making sure that Olga had departed, Theodore showed Bentley the garden. "It's beautiful, isn't it?"

"She's always had a green – ah, multi-colored – thumb."

"Has she always been so . . . . so . . . ." Theodore struggled to find the right word.

"Yes, she has," smiled Bentley, "though I'm not sure what to call it, either."

"Valkira has it, too."

"And we must never try to take it away from her!" Bentley looked sternly at Theodore. "When you get older, don't ever let anything make you forget that!"

"I understand, Sir," replied Theodore solemnly. And he really did.

The old man and the boy leaned back and listened to the garden, savoring their newfound companionship.

When Minerva and Valkira returned, everyone got to work on the Costume. While the cats supervised, Olga sat in her dacha, watching Bentley's every move.

After much measuring and cutting and sewing by flying fingers, Bentley went to try on the finished ensemble.

When he finally sauntered back out on the porch, Valkira clapped and cheered.

"*Très bien!*" said Katya and Koshka, with rather more enthusiasm than their Gallic souls usually allowed.

"Good show, Sir!" said Theodore sincerely.

And Minerva remembered what a fine figure of a man her husband had been. And still was, albeit somewhat larger around the middle.

Even Olga was unable to restrain her tail from wagging – but only in the dacha, where no one could see it.

Bentley was wearing a formal tuxedo – complete with tails – made of shiny silver cloth. Under the suit coat was a black turtleneck with a circular yin-yang symbol embroidered on his chest. On his head was a black derby, under his arm was a black umbrella; both were trimmed with silver sequins. And on his feet were black patent-leather tap shoes.

Bentley raised the umbrella and pushed its release. It flew up with a whoosh, lifting him a few inches off the ground. "In case I have to fly," he exclaimed, looking meaningfully at Olga scowling from her dacha.

"You'll need a mantra," said Theodore, watching his adopted grandfather levitate above the porch, "so you can instantly change in and out of your Costume."

Bentley descended, closed his umbrella, and tapped out an intricate series of steps worthy of Gene Kelly. *"Ta-Dah!"* he exclaimed, stopping dramatically, arms extended.

"Wow!" Theodore clapped appreciatively. "Really good show!"

"And now I want to see your Costumes," said Bentley, striking a dapper pose.

"Hoo . . . Hooo . . . .Hoooo . . . . ." And there was Theodore in all his feathered finery.

"Ohm . . . Ohmm . . . . Ohmmm . . . . ." Valkira exploded into her purple horned ensemble.

"Oh, I say . . . . Wonderful! Wonderful!" Bentley opened his umbrella and jauntily rose from the porch.

Valkira and Theodore leaped up and zoomed in circles around their grandfather.

"Grandmère, you need a Costume, too," said Valkira, swooping down.

"Yes, Minerva, all that brown is not very interesting," added Bentley, hovering overhead.

"I'm too old for that gold lamé cat-suit you seem to be remembering!" Minerva grinned, suddenly looking years younger.

"Oh, I'm not so sure about that . . . ." Bentley grinned back, with a much younger twinkle in his eye.

"Well," said Minerva finally, "I'll see what I can do." Spreading her cloak, she swirled around and yelled *"Shazam!"*

And there she stood, statuesque in a glittering gold garment, her hair cascading in unbound tresses down her back. Except for the skirt, her Costume was just like the jumpsuit so fondly remembered.

Bentley descended and offered his arm. As Minerva took it, her smile was as dazzling as her gown. Together, they slowly ascended and waltzed above the dancing flowers.

"Hurrah!" shouted Valkira and Theodore, soaring in happy loops around the hovering grandparents.

The gold-and-silver ring on Minerva's right hand suddenly reappeared on her left ring finger. And as she looked into his eyes, Bentley knew that he had finally been forgiven.

Chapter 14

Celebration

Minerva and Morgana were relaxing together on The Co-op bank's rooftop deck, surveying with satisfaction the scene below. All of the shops were back in business, and the gazebo had been rebuilt. The street had even been permanently closed to motor vehicles by an ordinance unanimously passed by the Town Council.

"They thought it was the least they could do after what happened," remarked Morgana, with a wry grin. "My guess is that some of them know who the perpetrators were."

"Or maybe were part of The Posse themselves?" wondered Minerva.

"Perhaps. In any case, the vicious attack on The Co-op boomeranged. Many people who'd never been here before came to help us rebuild. Including some of those men who 'forgot' to vote for me." Morgana paused and looked pointedly at Minerva. "And even I got my hands dirty."

Minerva smiled. "You should be very proud of what you've accomplished here," she said sincerely.

"Thank you," replied Morgana, obviously touched. "That's high praise – especially from you."

"I know some people who would like to hear about The Co-op – who might like to try it themselves." Minerva hesitated, eyeing Morgana carefully. "Will you come with me and tell them what you've done here?"

"When?" asked Morgana, without hesitation.

"Tomorrow."

"I'll be ready," said Morgana, again without hesitation.

"Olga and I will pick you up." Minerva was pleased.

The next morning, Olga landed especially carefully on the rooftop deck. Trying to act as though she did this sort of thing all the time, Morgana stepped – for the first time – into the sled. Olga took off extra smoothly.

After an extra-conservative flight, they approached The Sanctuary. As Olga circled for a landing, Morgana calmly regarded the various landmarks Minerva was pointing out. But when they pulled into the parking lot between Babushka Ekaterina's troika and Sophia's camel-driven chariot, Morgana began to have second thoughts. Especially when dog and horses greeted each other in exuberant Russian. Hastily she pulled out her pince-nez and nervously pretended to study them.

"Something wrong?" asked Minerva innocently, restraining a chuckle.

"Ah, no – no – er – I just don't understand Russian." Morgana climbed out of the sled with as much dignity as she could muster. Taking a deep breath, she followed Minerva to the castle.

Inside the coffeehouse, however, discomfort changed to fascination as she regarded the international décor and heard the harmonious blend of so many different tongues.

Minerva led Morgana to the center table and introduced her friends.

"Welcome," said Babushka Ekaterina warmly, enveloping her in a hearty Russian hug. "We've heard so much about you!"

Morgana, who normally did <u>not</u> hug, was surprised how easily she responded in kind.

She was even more surprised that she effortlessly understood all the languages in which the rest of the grandmothers questioned her. And that <u>they</u> understood <u>her</u>. They listened raptly as she described The Co-op, and nodded enthusiastically when Simone proposed they try it in their own towns.

"Suitably adapted, of course, to native tradition," said Shizuka, a seasoned hand at such things.

When Maria invited Morgana to visit her village as a consultant, the others also urged her to help them set up their own Co-ops. Morgana excitedly accepted.

At the end of the day, it was very clear that Morgana and the grandmothers were all speaking the same language – albeit with different accents. She was, accordingly, unanimously inducted into the International Order of Grandmothers.

Minerva, greatly pleased, grasped Morgana's hand as they all sang "The Grandmothers' Internationale." Morgana herself was not surprised that she already knew the words.

Ω Ω Ω

Minerva was waiting in front of the castle, hoping she hadn't made a huge mistake. Glancing at her friends, waiting beside her, did nothing to calm her apprehension. It had been hard enough convincing them to let Bentley make his first visit. And this time, he was bringing a whole busload of men! How had she let him talk her into such a foolhardy enterprise?!

"They're late!" snapped Babushka Ekaterina.

"Maybe they got lost," suggested Sophia, tapping her foot impatiently.

"And wouldn't stop to ask directions," added Simone, arching an eyebrow.

The butterflies in Minerva's stomach galloped wildly.

Ten minutes later, a school bus pulled up at the gate of The Sanctuary, and was nervously allowed to enter.

"ГрррЛ," Olga growled as the bus drove into the parking lot. The Troika horses neighed their disapproval in voluble Russian. Maria's burro and Sophia's camel also made disparaging noises, some of them quite rude.

As Bentley opened the door and alighted from the bus, Minerva stepped forward to greet him. She could see that he was as nervous as she was.

The other grandfathers got off the bus and lined up, trying unsuccessfully to act as though they did this sort of thing everyday.

The grandmothers stood in a line across from them, trying unsuccessfully to hide their distrust as they looked at the old men.

Finally, Babushka Ekaterina stepped forward. "It has to start somewhere," she said evenly. "So let's all have some tea."

She turned and walked into the castle, followed by the other women. Bentley motioned to the men, who walked behind, trying not to gawk too obviously.

In the coffeehouse, the grandmothers split up and reluctantly sat two to a table. The grandfathers had no choice but to join them – two to a table. Again, they tried – without success – not to gawk.

Minerva and Bentley sat at the center table with Babushka Ekaterina and the unofficial leader of the men's delegation. Maestro Vittorio was as passionately Italian as Babushka Ekaterina was Russian. After some preliminary verbal skirmishing, they each conceded that the other's mother tongue was one of the two best languages in which to sing. Soon, amid much dramatic gesturing and bursting into exuberant song, they were enjoying a friendly argument about the relative merits of Verdi and Tchaikovsky.

Minerva and Bentley excused themselves, and discreetly monitored the other tables, at which conversation was proceeding at varying stages of success and with various degrees of warmth – or lack thereof.

Sophia was attempting to make contact with a Japanese grandfather, who kept bowing while trying to avoid her gesturing hands. Simone and Vladimir were having a spirited discussion about Napoleon. Shizuka and Pedro were endeavoring to find middle ground between her subtle Asian reserve and his aggressive Latino machismo. Maria, meanwhile, was enjoying Maurice's stylish French manners as much as he was appreciating her wholehearted laughter at his tongue-in-cheek jokes.

And so it went, all over the room. Only occasionally did Minerva and Bentley feel compelled to mediate.

At the end of the afternoon, the grandfathers were as sorry to board the school bus as the grandmothers were to see it drive away.

At the next visit, a week later, the grandmothers were waiting eagerly in the parking lot. The grandfathers were smiling as they got off the bus.

And this time, they got down to business.

It was moved, seconded, and unanimously carried that the next meeting would be at The Retreat.

It was moved, seconded, and unanimously carried that they would bring their granddaughters and grandsons.

It was moved and seconded that the grandmothers would help the grandfathers make Costumes for themselves. There were several dissenting votes from the men, but "the ayes have it!"

The grinning grandmothers pushed the grumbling grandfathers onto the school bus, and they all headed for Fleur de Lily's. Once they met Lily, however, the grousing turned into delighted laughter as she helped them design their Costumes. Most of them went home with far more flamboyant outfits than the grandmothers would have conjured up on their own.

In tribute to Russian lyricism, Vittorio became a dashing Cossack. Bright blue loose-fitting pants were tucked into Italian leather boots; a glittering red tunic was covered with multi-colored spangles and belted with a silver-sequined belt. On his head was a Russian fur hat, lavishly trimmed with gold braid and a huge blue plume.

Vladimir was dressed as Napoleon. Though much too tall for the part, he nonetheless stuck his hand in his chest and struck an imperial pose. Hiro looked like a samurai warrior trying to be Zorro. Pedro looked like Zorro trying to be a samurai warrior. And Maurice wore a straw hat, carried a cane under his arm, and walked around singing "Mimi" and rolling his eyes.

All the men, of course, insisted on capes. "In case we have to fly," they said seriously. And the grandfathers proceeded to create the gaudiest, most ornate, thoroughly decorated capes imaginable. Every inch was emblazoned with every possible hue of sequins, spangles, braid and glitter.

"Let's hope they never have to," smirked Simone. "They'd never get airborne with all that stuff weighing them down."

"Shhhh," cautioned Minerva, trying not to giggle at the overdone cape Bentley had added to his Costume. "You'll spoil their fun."

The other grandmothers took heed and restrained their mirth.

Back at The Sanctuary, the women reluctantly got off the bus. And when it finally drove out of the parking lot, the school bus was painted with peace symbols and yin-yang circles. All the grandfathers were singing "We Shall Overcome" and Peace songs from the 60s.

Ω Ω Ω

This time it was Bentley who was waiting nervously at the gate. Never before had any female been welcomed to The Retreat.

Not all of the resident Patricians had approved the Peace Mission. More had come – secretly, at first – over to Bentley's side since his initial announcement, but at least as many were still opposed.

The first shock wave had hit The Retreat with the arrival of the grandsons. Each grandfather had brought only one – his best-behaved pre-adolescent – and had smuggled them in as unobtrusively as possible. However, even good boys will be boys, and there were some small – but unpleasant – incidents. Theodore, whom Bentley had brought early, did much to minimize the disruption.

The Retreat, of course, had a very efficient grapevine, so the traditional Patricians knew something bigger – and much worse – was afoot. For now, they were laying low – but on red alert.

All the grandmothers decided to fly. This was, after all, their usual mode of transport. And it would be a good reminder to the men that a mere gate could not have kept them out, if they had chosen to enter sooner.

Minerva was the first to arrive, Valkira sitting beside her in the sled. Olga made an especially graceful landing, and gave Bentley a defiant – but not entirely hostile – look.

Behind the sled flew the small train Morgana had appropriated from one of The Sanctuary's disassembled carnival rides. Ophelia sat next to her in the open passenger car. The locomotive was driven by Wolf, who had made a nearly full recovery. He did, of course, bear many scars – the worst of which was covered by an eye-patch Olga assured him was really quite debonair.

Following Wolf over the gate flew Ekaterina's troika, Sophia's chariot, Shizuka's economy hybrid, Maria on her burro, and all manner of other highly original, recycled conveyances. Last of all, Simone's hot air balloon floated dramatically over the gate, and landed on the stage of the outdoor amphitheatre. All of the grandmothers had brought granddaughters, most of whom were around Valkira's age. All of them looked curiously at The Retreat as they walked to the theatre benches and sat down. The grandsons, herded by Theodore, followed.

The crowd hushed as Bentley and the grandfathers walked out on the stage.

"Welcome to The Retreat!" he said, his voice shaking just enough to be noticeable. He caught Minerva's encouraging look, and continued with more confidence. "This is a very important occasion, one that we hope will be the first of many more cultural exchanges. We have lots of fun things to do so we can get acquainted. And there's lots of good food for when you get hungry. Then, later, we'll have some music and dancing."

Cheering and applause, enthusiastic but not rowdy.

"So now," shouted Bentley, raising both arms and making V's with his fingers, "everyone have a good time and make new friends!"

The grandsons went with the grandmothers for rides in their various vehicles, accompanied by much excited whooping. The granddaughters were teamed with grandfathers to play whimsical, non-competitive games to a draw. Delighted laughter filled the camp.

In between were snacks from booths dispensing food adored by grandkids, frowned on by grandmothers, but allowed by grandfathers eager to please. Valkira stuffed herself with hot dogs until her stomach ached.

Finally, they all returned, sweaty and full, to the amphitheatre. Various groups of old and young had prepared entertainment, and the audience was waiting for them to perform.

Suddenly, a large group of old men, wearing military uniforms and waving worn flags from the Great War, barged out onto the stage.

"This is indecent!" screamed their leader. "It's treason! It's blasphemy! Get these infidels and their unholy contraptions out of here!" The others started yelling with him.

Bentley jumped up on the stage and tried to calm them.

"You traitor! You brought all of THEM here!" shouted the Bald One. "How dare you call yourself a Patrician! You are no longer one of the Best People!"

"That's fine with me!" Bentley retorted. "I'd rather be one of the Good People!"

Minerva and Valkira and Theodore cheered and whistled and stamped their feet.

Ophelia, however, slowly climbed onto the stage and walked calmly toward the clamoring old men. Before their eyes, she transformed into her beautiful Costume, trailing flowers and fluttering veils. Softly she began to sing. One by one, the angry men stopped shouting, and the audience quieted down. On and on Ophelia sang, her sweet music filling their hearts and wrapping gently around them. As her song evoked poignant memories of comrades fallen in the Great War, they sank to their knees, tears streaming unheeded. Some of the grandmothers appeared next to them, and put comforting arms on shaking shoulders.

When Ophelia stopped singing, there was absolute silence.

Finally, Minerva stood and addressed the whole group. "Now we are ALL Good People!" And she led them in a moving rendition of "The Grandparents Internationale."

Arise! Ye grandparents strong
Who want to right what is wrong.
Stand up now
And proclaim how
And sing our marching song.

For our grandchildren's sake,
It is time to awake!
Let's seize the hour
For Senior power
And make the world quake!

"And now," said Bentley, standing beside her, "Let's celebrate!"

Dozens of musical instruments struck up the band. Fireworks exploded overhead.

"Ohm . . . Ohmm . . . . Ohmmm . . . . ." Valkira shot into the air like a purple rocket.

"Hoo . . . Hooo . . . . Hoooo . . . . ." Theodore spread his wings and flew up next to her.

"Ta-Dah!" shouted Bentley, tapping in a rapid circle. His umbrella whooshed open and up he floated.

"Shazam!" Minerva swirled and took his outstretched hand as she ascended.

All around them grandchildren were shouting mantras, exploding into whimsical Costumes, and zooming over the amphitheatre. Many of the grandmothers climbed into their vehicles and joined them. The grandfathers tried unsuccessfully to fly, most of them refusing to shed their heavy capes. Olga took pity and ferried them up and around in her sled.

The old men on the stage watched, amazed, thinking about their own grandchildren – and hoping that they, too, might still have good times together.

Everyone else sang joyously. The world out there was still standing on its head. But here and now, Alpha and Omega had joined to celebrate the Circle of Life.